Real Mermaids

DON'T SELL SEASHELLS

HÉLÈNE BOUDREAU

sourcebooks
jabberwocky

Published by Sourcebooks Jabberwocky, an imprint of Sourcebooks, Inc.
P.O. Box 4410, Naperville, Illinois 60567-4410
(630) 961-3900
Fax: (630) 961-2168
www.jabberwockykids.com

Library of Congress Cataloging-in-Publication Data is on file with the pub-
lisher.

Source of Production: Victor Graphics, Baltimore, Maryland
Date of Production: December 2013
Run Number: 22127

Printed and bound in the United States of America.
VG 10 9 8 7 6 5 4 3 2 1

For my Markham Bahama Mamas: Andrea, Chantal, Peggy, Renée, Sara, and Tracey

Chapter One

I NEVER REALIZED I WAS afraid of flying until I was hurtling through space at a kajillion miles an hour on my way to my mom and dad's beachside tropical wedding.

"Um, Jade?" My best friend, Cori, leaned over and whispered in my ear from 16B, the airplane seat beside me. "You okay?"

The "Fasten Seat Belts" light dinged, and my stomach dropped as the airplane hit turbulence for the umpteenth time. The smelly toddler behind me kept bashing into my headrest, and the lady in front of me had *her* seat reclined all the way back, adding to the claustrophobic feeling of the flight.

Plus, I had a feeling Stinky Pants had a doo-doo in his diaper because that wasn't the food cart I was smelling.

Perfect.

"Yeah, I'm totally okay," I replied in the most convincing voice I could manage. *Okay? I should be ecstatic.* We were on our way to the Eutopia Resort in the Bahamas so my mom and dad could finally tie the knot and make our family official. "Couldn't be better. Why do you ask?"

"Um," Cori said, "because your fingernails are digging into me and I think you're about to draw blood." She winced, looking down at her arm pinned to the armrest.

"Oh! Sorry!" I released my death grip and glanced at the flickering red images from the television screen on the back of the seat in front of me, which was tilted at an awkward angle thanks to Miss Snore-A-Lot in 15A. "The, uh… movie is just really intense."

Cori shook her arm to get the blood flowing again and leaned over to check my screen. "You're watching Elmo."

"Right." I'd tried to find something to watch earlier to keep my mind occupied but got distracted by the fact I was basically putting my life into the hands of a pilot I'd never met.

I drew in a few deep breaths, trying to get oxygen to my brain, and glanced down at my frayed jeans, green Chuck Taylor sneakers, and my favorite oversized "Achin' for the Bacon" T-shirt, compared to Cori's funky seashell-beaded tank top and graphic flowery-print skirt, which she'd matched with gold gladiator sandals. Like always, Cori had dressed for style and I had dressed for comfort.

Only, the joke was on me because I was *anything* but comfortable.

"I know it's Elmo," I continued, "but he just lost his puppy and he's sad. Very, very sad."

I scanned the seats in front of me and spotted Mom and Dad in row 14. Their heads were tilted toward one another, probably making last-minute wedding plans about flowers or refreshments or music. Everything about the trip had been so last minute that they were still trying to pull together all the details for the wedding. But I'd never seen them happier than during the past few weeks, since Mr. Chamberlain presented us with official passports from his secret source. Those passports finally made us legitimate human beings rather than just underwater sea creatures with an identity crisis.

"Does Elmo even have a puppy?" Cori looked at me through narrowed eyes. "You're freaked out about something, aren't you?"

The plane hit turbulence (again!), making the flight attendant stumble a bit, but he braced a hand on the back of one of the seats and smiled brightly, then continued handing out packages of stale pretzels as if nothing had happened.

He didn't fool me. We were going down with the plane—straight into the watery depths of the Caribbean Sea. I felt it in my gut. Even for a part-time mermaid like me, that didn't sound like a very healthy prospect.

Taking a lesson from the flight attendant, I turned to Cori with a smile plastered on my face.

"Me? Freaked out? No…"

Just then, Stinky Pants's mom stood up and whacked the headrest into the back of my skull as she struggled to carry her toddler to the closet-sized bathroom to (hopefully) change his diaper.

"Is it all the gossip you were telling me about back home?" Cori asked as I rubbed the back of my head. "You know people just need stuff to talk about because their own lives are so boring, right?"

It was true—the Port Toulouse rumor mill had kicked into high gear since news spread about the reason for our trip.

Did you hear? Dalrymple Baxter is marrying his dead wife's sister!

I'd overheard a few women at Dooley's Drugstore saying how scandalous the wedding between my dad and my "aunt" was. Most of Port Toulouse thought Mom had drowned in a swimming accident at Gran's cottage the year before. Little did they know that my "Tanti Natasha" was actually Mom's secret identity to cover up the fact that she's a mermaid and very much alive!

"That's kind of a bummer, but no," I replied. The upcoming Baxter wedding might seem sketchy to people who didn't know better. But like Dad said, we'd cope with the whispers and finger-pointing when we got back.

"Is it because I came with you guys a few days early since my mom couldn't get time off work?" Cori persisted.

Cori's parents had jumped at the invitation to join us because Mrs. Blake and Mom had been best friends since Cori and I were toddlers. But the Blakes couldn't meet up with us until Friday, just in time for the Saturday wedding.

In fact, not everyone could come on our trip. Serena was spending our weeklong fall school break underwater with her mer-parents and Gran was nervous about flying because of her pacemaker, so I was totally pumped that Cori could come early and that our friends (slash boyfriends),

Luke and Trey, would be flying down with their parents at the end of the week too.

"No, of course not," I insisted. "I'm glad you're here."

"'Cause I totally could have waited to come with my parents, but I kind of couldn't wait to get out of Port Toulouse," Cori said. "Oh, geesh. Now I feel like an idiot. You guys have never flown anywhere together before, especially out of the country. Am I creeping on your family time?"

It was true about never flying out of the country. The main reason was because Mom never had a passport or paperwork proving she was human, since she, um, actually wasn't. Now that she was legit as far as the government was concerned, thanks to Mr. Chamberlain, it opened up a whole new world of possibility, which was awesome!

And scary.

"It's not that," I insisted. "But hold on a sec—why couldn't you wait to get out of Port Toulouse?"

"Ah, just something stupid," Cori said.

Cori had slept over at my house the night before so we could leave early for the airport that morning, and I knew she and Trey had been texting until late. "Does this have something to do with Trey?" I asked, taking a few deep, cleansing breaths to keep my mind off the fact we were flying on top of the clouds.

Not natural!

"It's nothing, and don't change the subject," Cori said.

"I'm just changing the subject because you're changing the subject!" I retorted but I made the mistake of glancing through the airplane window. I instantly regretted it because my stomach started pitching like a dinghy on the open sea. I slammed the window blind shut.

"Oh!" Cori's eyes popped open in realization. "You're afraid of flying, aren't you?"

I stuffed the last few stale pretzels in my mouth and crumpled up the bag. "It would help if they had better snacks."

"You're unbelievable." Cori laughed and shook her head.

"What?" I demanded. It was easy for her—her family had flown to tons of places: Florida a few times during spring break and once to British Columbia where they boarded a cruise ship to Alaska.

"Sorry. I'm not making fun of you, but think about it!" Cori leaned over and whispered. "You took down an underwater empire full of Mermish baddies a few weeks ago, and now you're afraid of a teensy-weensy airplane?"

"Maybe?" I said quietly.

"Listen," Cori continued, "you're just paranoid about everything these days, which is understandable considering what you've been through this year. But trust me, danger isn't lurking around every corner. Not everyone is out to get you, remember?"

Cori had a point. The last few months had been the craziest of my life. I'd learned I was part mermaid and found out my mother hadn't drowned. I'd finally freed Mom from Talisman Lake, so she could find the hidden tidal pool that would help her become human again. In the meantime, I'd started dating a boy (Luke) who turned out to be a mer-boy too, and together we helped bring democracy to the underwater mers off the coast of Port Toulouse.

With all that behind me, I should be able to just relax and enjoy a vacation with my friends and family, shouldn't I?

"You're right." I took a deep breath and tried to relax. "I know you're right."

"Do me a favor," Cori said cheerily. "For the next week, pretend mermaids are just mythical creatures like vampires and zombies. You're dry, on land, and human, and nobody is out to get you. Make that your mantra, okay?"

"Dry. On land. Human. Got it," I said quietly, putting my earbuds in and trying to find a TV channel that didn't involve Muppets so I could distract myself for the rest of the trip.

"Cool." Cori pulled the airplane blanket up to her chin and rested her head on my shoulder. Soon, she was sleeping like a baby and, ugh, drooling all over my shirt.

I shifted in my seat, trying to get comfortable. Maybe Cori was right. Maybe I'd gotten so used to things going wrong and danger splashing out at me from every corner that I didn't even know how to live a normal life anymore.

Meanwhile, Stinky Pants and his mom settled back into their seats behind me, smelling a whole lot fresher, and Miss Snore-A-Lot finally woke up and brought her seat forward.

Maybe things *were* looking up!

Or…maybe not.

Especially not, since the airplane seemed to start to nose-dive into the ocean!

I gripped the armrests as we started plummeting to our watery graves just as the seat belt and "No Smoking" signs flashed on and a message rang out over the speaker:

Ladies and gentlemen, we are beginning our descent into Nassau, Bahamas.

Perfect. So we weren't nosediving into the ocean after all—just crash-landing onto the runway probably.

And not a moment too soon.

Chapter Two

I DON'T THINK I EVER appreciated the feeling of solid ground quite as much as when we finally landed in the Bahamas and I felt the steadiness of the Nassau airport's tiled floor beneath my feet.

I could feel the blood returning to my extremities as we made our way through the terminal, enjoying fruity-tasting complimentary beverages and soothing steel-drum music. We collected our suitcases from the baggage carousel, got a few maps from the tourism counter, and found the spot outside the terminal where our hotel's shuttle van was supposed to pick us up.

"How long until the shuttle?" I asked Dad as I felt the warm Caribbean sun against my cheeks.

"The what?" Dad squinted at me through his standard-issue geek glasses and worked his jaw like he was trying to get his ears to pop after the flight.

"The shuttle, honey!" Mom yelled so Dad could hear then turned to me and smiled. "The doctor said he'd be okay to fly, but I'm afraid his swimmer's ear is acting up again. He hasn't been able to understand two words since our descent. Anyway, the shuttle should be here any minute now."

"In it how? In what?" Dad yelled. Leave it to Dad to get swimmer's ear after one pool party at the Blakes' despite the fact his own wife and daughter had just spent *months* underwater as mermaids. Dad had been through so much, though, and really deserved this vacation. I reached an arm around him and gave him a hug.

"Stick with me, Dad. We can get matching lounge chairs by the hotel pool." Because there was no way I was actually going *in* the pool. Swimmer's ear or not, I planned to stay high and dry for the next six days. "Me and you, okay? Side by side."

"Ride? Is our ride here?" Dad asked, looking down the Arrivals platform.

"Not yet, honey." Mom patted Dad's arm and shrugged at me with a smile.

Families milled around the taxi stands and shuttle stops with their rolling suitcases, pointing at local landmarks on half unfolded maps, and I could feel a weird sense of calm as the air crackled with the excitement and optimism Cori had promised back on the plane.

"Okay, I'm starting to tune into the island vibe now," I said to Cori as the palm trees swayed around us.

The warm Caribbean air was a welcome change compared to our chilly October days back in Port Toulouse. I could imagine myself lying on the beach and catching up on the latest celebrity gossip magazines, now that I had escaped the flying death trap.

"I know, right?" Cori agreed. "And it's still early, so we have the rest of the day ahead of us. Wait until you get to the Eutopia resort. My mom and dad went there for their tenth anniversary and showed me pictures. The beach has amazingly soft, white sand, and the buffets have the biggest shrimp you've ever seen." She considered this for a second. "Well, the biggest shrimp *I've* ever seen, anyway."

"I think I could get used to this," I said, closing my eyes to fully enjoy the moment.

This is what *normal* people did—go on vacations, buy lame souvenirs, and read trashy magazines under a hot blazing sun.

Ahh, so relaxing…

Until, that was, we put our lives into the hands of the crazy lady with a death wish behind the wheel of our hotel's shuttle van.

"Whoa!" Cori and I squeezed ourselves between two sticky boys with lollipops at the back of the shuttle van and had to keep dodging their death wands as they waved the lollipops in the air and shot *Avada Kedavra* curses at each other. I was beginning to understand why the boys' parents had ditched them in the back of the van with us and nabbed seats behind the driver.

"Hello, everyone! My name is Faye and I'll be your driver today." Faye's mirrored sunglasses flashed up at us in her rearview mirror and her cheery smile gleamed white against her dark brown skin. The van was jam-packed with passengers and luggage, and it even looked like the front passenger seat was occupied.

Whiffs of breath mints and stale coffee filled the air, but at least Faye didn't smoke. Otherwise, with her wicked race-car-driver-like reflexes and the fact we were packed in there like sardines, I'd be adding another aroma to the van of the "upchuckity" kind that no amount of minty freshness could mask.

We zipped through the island streets, past a mix of newer hotels and pockets of rundown-looking houses and buildings, while Faye rattled off the sightseeing highlights between jokes and local gossip.

"…and off in the distance you can see the twin towers of the Eutopia Resort, which was made famous by movies like *To Catch a Spy* and *The Forgiveness Diaries* starring Sean Diggory," Faye said.

I could barely keep up with what she was saying in her mile-a-minute Caribbean accent. Plus, the only things I saw were blurred buildings and snatches of the ocean whizzing by my window. I wouldn't be surprised if our shuttle van driver was related to our airplane pilot.

"That's where we'll be staying." Mom pointed to the Eutopia Resort and grinned. I gripped the metal bar across the back of her seat and tried to keep from sliding into one of the Sticky Boys as Faye took a corner at warp speed.

"And to the left is the island's famous Straw Market where local artisans sell their wares," Faye continued. "The new Straw Market building had some flooding problems in last week's storm, so the booths are temporarily relocated at the waterfront near Señor Frog's, but the market is a must for visitors to the island, so make sure you take that in during your stay."

This was definitely the touristy part of town. The tumbledown shacks and narrow alleys were gone, replaced by high-end shops selling jewelry, perfume, and clothes.

"Oh," Cori exclaimed between waving lollipops, "Lainey said we should totally go to the Straw Market. She got this really cool conch ring from one of the booths when she was here with her parents last year but lost it, so I promised I'd try to find her another one."

Lainey Chamberlain and I had never been the best of friends, but we'd struck a truce at the Fall Folly dance after she'd discovered her own father's mer secret. While Lainey might never become my best bud, it was nice to see Cori talking to her again since they both loved fashion and Cori had long since given up on improving my "shabby chic" style.

I leaned over the seat in front of me and whispered to Dad. "Does this lady's pay get docked for every minute she's late dropping us off?"

"What did you drop? Want me to get it for you?" Dad yelled and hunted under his seat.

"No, it's okay, Dalrymple. And no need to yell..." Mom patted Dad on the back and he bumped his head on the seat's crossbar as he sat back up. Mom cringed. "It's just over that bridge, Jade. Not long now."

We crossed the long bridge separating Nassau and

Paradise Island, and I got my first good look at the blue Caribbean waters. I could see three huge cruise ships docked along the piers, all gleaming white and cheery.

"I wonder—" I caught Cori's eye and waved a hand in front of me in a fishy, mermaid-tail motion.

"Jade, we talked about this, remember? Dry, on land," she said then mouthed *and human* so the others wouldn't hear.

"Yeah, yeah. I remember." But with all the beautiful, crystal blue waters surrounding us, I had a feeling I'd need more than a three-line mantra to switch from mermaid mode to vacation mode.

Once we got to the other side of the bridge, the shuttle van wove its way through the smooth streets and manicured grounds of Paradise Island and Faye dropped the first couple at their hotel. I thought the hotel was called "the Asylum," though as we got closer to the sign, I could tell someone had rearranged the letters and it was actually the Alyssum. It looked nice enough, though the balconies all looked out onto the parking lot and I thought I saw a group of college-aged frat boys going through the lobby with blow-up dinosaurs around their waists.

After traveling a few more streets by pristine grounds, manicured lawns, and perfectly shaped shrubs, we arrived at the Eutopia Resort. Faye pulled the van up to the glittering lobby doors, stopping next to a super-long stretch Hummer limousine.

"Isn't that Taylor 'n Tyler?" Cori jumped up and down

in her seat and pointed to an extremely tanned, bleached, and sunglassed young man and woman all dressed in white.

"As in the singers Taylor 'n Tyler?" I asked. Taylor Ariella and Tyler Green had been the "It" couple of the pop music scene for the past year. They'd recently collaborated on an album that had hit platinum in its first week of being released. But what were the odds that we'd be booked in the same hotel as the famous duo that had been on every cover of every entertainment magazine in the past six months? "Nah…what are the chances?"

The Taylor 'n Tyler look-alikes and their entourage were escorted into the lobby by two hotel staff members who came out to greet them.

Dad and Mom and the other adults got out of the shuttle van first, while Cori and I managed to clamber out from the backseat, but not before one of the Sticky Boys' lollipops got stuck in my hair and I was left with a gooey grape glob hanging from my ponytail.

"You guys wait here while I go check on our reservation!" Dad yelled to us as he went into the lobby while Mom helped unglue the lollipop from my hair and Sticky Boy #1 screamed his head off because I "stoled" his treat.

"Well, if he hadn't tried to *Wingardium Leviosa* his brother out of the van, his lollipop wand might not have gotten stuck in my hair," I muttered to Mom as she tried to untangle the goopy mess.

"Not to worry. I think that's all of it," Mom said as she wiped her hands with a wet wipe from the plane.

"Thanks, Mom."

Faye was just finishing unloading all the bags from the back of the van. She plunked my Dalmatian-print rolling suitcase next to me. "No way you're gonna lose that one, are you, honey?" she asked kindly.

"It was a gift from my grandmother," I replied with a smile, remembering how Gran had gone to three different stores with me to help pick out a suitcase. She'd felt bad she couldn't come but wanted to send me off to the Bahamas in style.

"You have a Dalmatian?" Faye asked. "My granddaughter Rayelle has always wanted one. Ever since she was a little girl and saw that Dalmatian movie. Not so little anymore." She chuckled. "Rayelle, dear. Come out and say hi, sweetie."

That's when I noticed that the passenger in the front seat still hadn't gotten out of the van. The door opened and Rayelle unfolded herself from the front seat. She looked like she was a year or so older than Cori and me, and had tight dark curls and long brown legs. *Really* long legs.

"Hi!" Cori was the first to stick out her hand to introduce herself. "I'm Cori and this is Jade."

"Hi," the girl said quickly.

"Rayelle's just hitching a ride from school to her mama's work at the Straw Market. She doesn't have a school break in the fall like you lucky girls," Faye said. "You all like shopping?"

Cori's ears perked up like a puppy's do when you ask if it wants to go for a walk. "I *love* shopping."

"Well, if you can be ready, my next stop here is in an

hour. I'll be swinging back by the Straw Market and can drop you off on the way back to the airport," Faye said as she shut her van's back door.

"Oh, could we?" Cori turned to my mom.

I eyed Cori's celebrity magazines. Honestly, the only thing I wanted to do for the rest of the afternoon was find a lounge chair next to the pool and park myself there until I was all caught up on the Brangelinas and Taylor 'n Tylers of the celebrity world. I could only hope that the lollipop boys were not going to be anywhere near our room because their Sticky Boy antics were starting to make my head ache.

"I don't see why not," Mom replied with a smile.

Foiled.

"Perfect then. And call me anytime you need a ride anywhere on the island." Faye fished a few business cards from her pocket and gave them to each of us. I stuffed mine in my bag.

"I'll be at my mom's booth," Rayelle said. "Come find me and I can give you a tour." "Excellent!" Cori said, rolling her hot pink suitcase onto the sidewalk beside me.

By then, a group of hotel guests going back to the airport had accumulated, and Faye and Rayelle busied themselves reloading the back of the van with luggage. Soon, they were all packed up and Faye tooted her horn as they drove away.

"I wonder what's keeping your dad." Mom looked over her shoulder at the reception area. "Are you guys okay here if I go check on him?"

"Sure," I replied, sitting on my Dalmatian-print suitcase.

"Once we get all settled in our rooms, we can catch the shuttle back to the Straw Market. Maybe we can find some cute sarongs for the wedding and a beachy tropical shirt for your dad. All he brought are T-shirts," Mom said as she pushed through the lobby doors and disappeared inside.

"We should find out about this paddleboarding excursion," Cori said, looking through a brochure she'd nabbed at the airport tourist kiosk. "And windsurfing. And sea kayaking. Oh, and they have this thing called Snuba diving!"

So much for my plan to chillax.

That's when Sticky Boy #2 upchucked all over my Chuck Taylor sneakers.

Chapter Three

TURNED OUT (AFTER DITCHING my beloved "upchucked" Chucks, washing my feet in the ocean, and rooting through my luggage to find a pair of flip-flops) that the Eutopia Resort didn't have a record of our reservation after all.

"You have no room for us?" Dad yelled. I wasn't sure if he was yelling because he was angry or because his ears were still blocked from the airplane, but either way, people looked over from the hotel lobby bar and a burly-looking security guard came over to investigate the situation.

"Sir, there is no reservation on file for a Dalrymple Baxter. I've checked several times," the hotel attendant said, looking up from her computer.

"I'd bet you any money that Taylor 'n Tyler and their entourage stole our reservation," Cori whispered to me as we saw the large group of tanned, bleached, sunglassed people follow an army of bellhops pushing carts full of Gucci and Prada luggage toward the bank of elevators.

"Do you really think that's them?" I asked, squinting through the crowded lobby.

Cori flipped open an *OK!* Magazine to a photograph of Taylor Ariella holding an oversized bag with a dust mop of a puppy in it. It was the same kind of dog our "Taylor" was carrying in her handbag.

"That doesn't prove anything," I said, inspecting the picture, though it sure did look like her. "Those guys over there could just be some rich kids on school break."

But still, if Taylor 'n Tyler and their crew *did* get us kicked out of our hotel, that was so *not* cool.

"But I have the confirmation number right here!" Dad continued to yell, showing the paper he'd brought with him from our travel agent with all the reservation information.

"I'm sorry, sir," the hotel attendant repeated for the umpteenth time while signaling for the security guard, "but your yelling is upsetting the other guests and there really isn't anything else I can do for you. I'm afraid I'm going to have to ask you to leave."

The refrigerator-sized security guard sprang into action and started loading our luggage onto a cart to escort us out the door.

"Number! Confirmation number!" Dad insisted, waving the paper in the air.

"Come on, Dalrymple," Mom said quietly, taking his arm. "We'll figure something else out."

After a series of phone calls to our travel agent, which probably cost as much in cell-phone fees as the plane tickets to the Bahamas, we finally got rebooked at a smaller hotel down the road.

"The Asylum?" I said as we rolled our suitcases up

the driveway after walking the half mile or so from the Eutopia. The straps of my flip-flops were already starting to make my feet ache.

"A side of what?" Dad asked, tapping the side of his head with the heel of his hand as though trying to dislodge something from his ear canal.

"The Alyssum," Mom yelled to Dad, giving me a look. "It's a type of flower."

"Oh," he replied, still not looking like he'd heard what she said. Honestly, he'd be screaming his vows if his ears didn't get unplugged in time for the wedding.

"Well, judging by that gang of college frat boys I saw earlier, it might as well be an asylum," I said.

"As long as there's a pool and a beach, that's all we need, right?" Cori asked brightly.

"Exactly. It'll be fine," Mom reassured me. "But since the Eutopia lost all our reservations, I need to rebook all the wedding plans too. The flowers, the wedding officiate to perform the ceremony, the music—I don't know how I'm going to get it all done in time."

I gave myself twenty mental lashes for being such a dork. Mom needed me to step up to the plate and help her out with the wedding, not complain about something we didn't have any control over.

"We'll help you. Don't worry." I put my arm around her as we walked through the lobby, trying to reassure her.

"Yeah, I bet we can find lots of stuff at the Straw

Market for decorations," Cori suggested. "Isn't this the other hotel where Faye stopped on her way to our old hotel? We can still catch a ride with her if we hurry."

Mom smiled and glanced over to Dad as he got us checked in to our rooms. The clerk at the registration desk looked wide-eyed as Dad yelled out our names to him, making sure he'd spelled them correctly.

"Maybe I'll send Dad into town with you to keep him out of trouble," Mom suggested, "and I'll stay back at the hotel to see if they can help us pull this wedding together in time for Saturday."

"Sounds like a plan," I agreed.

We grabbed a quick bite before the hotel staff finished clearing up the lunch buffet and managed to catch Faye on her next run to the airport. Faye dropped Cori, Dad, and me off at the top of the lane leading down to the waterfront, where we met Rayelle so we could all walk down to the Straw Market together.

"My run to the airport should have me back here at about five. Okay?" Faye called out from the driver's seat.

"Don't worry, Mamie. I have my phone if we need you," Rayelle called out to her as we started down the lane.

"Remind me to look for a ring for Lainey, and I hope I can find one of those Pandora knockoff bracelets, and oh, do you think they'll have Gucci purses?" she asked Rayelle.

"I think Cori has found her people," I joked with Dad.

"Yeah, lots and lots of people here, eh?" Dad said as he nodded toward the crowds of tourists weaving in and out of market stalls. His hearing was starting to come back but he was still losing a bit in translation.

"I'm just trying to absorb as much of the local culture as I can. Oh, cute!" Cori said as she skipped ahead. A huge, green frog statue greeted us at an ocean-side restaurant called Señor Frog's at the beginning of the market's booths.

"That's the biggest frog I've ever seen," I said, following close on her heels.

"I wonder if they have fancy drinks with umbrellas!" Dad said.

"I bet they do," I said with a smile. Dad had been joking for days that he couldn't wait to get away from his work as an engineer and sit by the ocean with a fancy tropical drink. "Why don't you sit on the balcony by the harbor and order one while Cori, Rayelle, and I look around the market?"

The stalls of the Straw Market stretched along the waterfront from Señor Frog's onward for a full city block.

"I don't know," Dad said skeptically. "It's not like we're in Port Toulouse anymore. What if you get lost?"

"Don't worry, Mr. Baxter. They'll be completely safe with me," Rayelle said, trying to reassure him.

"Oh look!" Cori climbed onto a massive yellow Adirondack chair in the front of the restaurant. The chair looked like it could fit all four of us comfortably. "Get on, guys! I'll ask that man over there to take our picture."

Cori hopped off the chair and was halfway down the sidewalk, about to ask a touristy-looking middle-aged guy to take our picture with her phone, when Rayelle chased after her and grabbed her arm.

"Are you crazy?" Rayelle asked.

"What?" Cori's eyes widened.

"You can't just go around asking any random guy to take your picture. He could take off with your phone or hassle you, or who knows what," Rayelle said. "So, keep your phone and wallet zipped up in a pocket of your bag and don't set it down anywhere."

"I thought you just told my dad it was completely safe," I said.

Dad looked from Rayelle to me to Cori, trying to follow our conversation.

"It is! But you don't have to be stupid about it," Rayelle said.

I was a bit surprised at how blunt Rayelle was, but I decided her no-BS approach was kind of nice compared to some gossip hounds I knew back in Port Toulouse who were nice enough to your face but talked trash about you behind your back. Like those ladies yammering about Mom and Dad at Dooley's Drugstore, for instance.

Dad must have thought so too, because he smiled brightly at Rayelle as though he'd gotten the gist of what we were talking about.

"Well, it sounds like you're in good hands," Dad said, taking a seat on Señor Frog's patio. "Enjoy your shopping and meet me back here in an hour."

"Oh," Cori said as we stepped down from Señor Frog's patio onto the busy Straw Market sidewalk. "Is there a place where we can get our hair braided?"

"Yeah," I pulled my ponytail over my shoulder, inspecting all the split ends. "Do you think my hair would stay in braids? I've always wanted to do that."

"My cousin braids hair on the beach by your hotel," Rayelle said. "I can take you there tomorrow if you want."

"That would be great!" Cori said.

A group of young people walked around with shell necklaces, trying to attach them around our necks.

"A gift from our island," one of the girls said.

"Oh, thank you. That's so nice." I moved my hair over so she could attach the necklace.

"Buzz off, Charla," Rayelle said, coming to my side. She whispered in my ear, "They only tell you it's free and then guilt you into buying it. Among other things."

"Oh," I said, feeling stupid.

Charla gave Rayelle a sneering look.

"You're so brave here with your boyfriend nearby, huh, Raybies? Get a grip." Charla nudged one of her friends and laughed at her own joke then headed off to find another customer.

"Charming girl. How do you know her?" I asked.

"Just a girl from school." Rayelle grabbed my arm to come with her. She looked over her shoulder as we walked and muttered. "Going nowhere fast."

"The necklace business must be good because that is either a very expensive watch she's wearing or an excellent knockoff," Cori whispered to me as we continued along the main strip.

"Any other Straw Market secrets we should know about?" I asked. I wasn't much of a shopper but maybe I could find the perfect vacation T-shirt to add to my extensive ratty T-shirt collection. Then I could really say, "Been there. Got the T-shirt!" if anyone asked if I'd ever been to the Bahamas.

"Just look at everything first before you buy it because you can get the same thing at different places for different prices. My mama's booth is at the other end." Rayelle led the way through the lane of colorful booths lining the Straw Market until we reached her mom's. She was a younger version of Faye and was busy embroidering a flower on a straw fan.

"That's really pretty," Cori said.

"Thank you, dear," Rayelle's mom said. "Things are a bit slow for now, Rayelle. Why don't you show your new friends around?"

"Thanks, Mama. I won't be long."

I tried to keep up with Rayelle and Cori as we squeezed around booths filled with glass-beaded bracelets, bobble-headed tin painted turtles, and straw wall hangings, but those girls were on a mission. I spotted a gray jersey T-shirt with a picture of the globe being sprinkled with peas that said "Peas on Earth" and thought I might actually buy something on this trip, but there were none in my size, reminding me why I hated shopping. Drat.

A flash of blue water appeared on my right between the booths where several water taxis waited for passengers. Peach and ivory conch shells were lined up on a colorful woven blanket along the edge of the pier. The shells reminded me of Mom and the Mermish stuff we'd been through in the past couple of months. She would probably really love those for the wedding, I decided.

"Cori, what do you think?" I asked, motioning to the shells. But I'd lost her in a jungle of knockoff Gucci and Chanel purses.

"I think I may have died and gone to Accessory Heaven," Cori said as she peeked out between draping fabrics. She pulled a hand-dyed bathing-suit cover-up from the rack and wrapped it around her waist. "Oh, this one would look amazing with the purple bikini I brought. Or do you think this one would be better?" She pointed to a tie-dyed version of the same thing.

"You're asking me? You must be desperate."

"You're right—I'll ask Rayelle," Cori replied with a joking smile. Then she turned when a teal wrap caught her eye. "Or maybe this one!"

"I can see this is going to take a while," I replied, trying not to sound too bored. Cori was having a blast and who was I to rain on her parade? Especially since it sounded like she was trying to get her mind off the Trey situation she'd left back home. "I'm going back there to look at those shells. Be back in five."

I backtracked a few booths and squeezed through the

narrow passage that led to the edge of the pier. Only one canopied water taxi remained, bobbing at its lines. The driver called out to see if I needed a ride.

"No thanks!" I waved to him and smiled.

He shoved off and sailed toward another part of the water-front to try his luck somewhere else just as a cruise ship blew its long, loud horn, practically scaring me out of my flip-flops. I took a deep breath to get my heart rate back to normal.

Sheesh, I was jumpy. But what was there to be jumpy about? I was on school break, on an awesome tropical vacation, with a great friend and a new one too.

Life was good.

I crouched to get a better look at the collection of conch shells laid out on the colorful cloth. The edges of the cloth flapped in the warm tropical breeze.

"Five dollars each, three for fifteen."

"That's not a deal." I turned to see the source of the voice.

"Dillon's Treasures, best deals in the market," said a bored-looking teenage guy with dreadlocks, sitting on a ripped lawn chair leaned up in the shade of the back of one of the Straw Market stalls. "And rich girls like you should know you get what you pay for."

"What makes you think I'm rich? And how do I know these are even yours?" I asked good-naturedly. "Are you Dillon?"

"The one and only," he muttered. A toothpick traveled from one side of his mouth to the other.

I picked up a shell and wondered how many I might

need for the wedding when I heard the sound of something calling over the water. Was it a dolphin? I'd never seen one near Port Toulouse so I was really hoping I'd get a chance this trip. Cori was totally gung ho to see a dolphin on one of the Snuba diving excursions offered at the hotel, but I was hoping to catch a glimpse of one from the safety of land, thank you very much.

"Do you have dolphins around here?" I asked. "I thought I heard something."

Dillon peeked an eye out from under his hat.

"I didn't hear nothing," he muttered.

I shaded my eyes from the sun with one hand and looked over the water to see if I could spot a dolphin surfacing, but all I saw were a few whitecaps over the tropical water. When I heard the sound again, I realized it was a man's voice from the passing cruise ship.

"That's a person, not a dolphin, by the way," Dillon said.

"Yeah, I kinda figured that out." I spotted the man in one of the lower portholes of the cruise ship, pushing something out of the porthole and into the ocean. It fell into the water with a big splash.

"And that's definitely not a dolphin either. *That's* a body!" Dillon yelled.

Chapter Four

A BODY! BEING THROWN OVERBOARD?
At least I *thought* it was a body. Legs, arms, a head—plunging toward the water from the porthole, followed by a sickening splash.

Yes! A body.

Or was it...

"Emergency! Emergency!" I yelled. I had no idea if that was what you were supposed to yell after you thought you saw a body being (possibly) thrown overboard from a cruise ship, but it blurted out of my mouth like a voice-over from one of those burglar alarm commercials on TV. "Someone call 911!"

Dillon's lawn chair toppled over as he stood. He pushed his dreadlocks away from his face and adjusted his hat. "You saw that too, right?"

It was amazing that we'd seen anything. It had all happened in a split second.

"You really think that was a body?" I asked, glancing at the harbor then back at him.

But by then, Dillon had disappeared like a phantom between the booths of the Straw Market. My heart pounded like a jackhammer. Now I was all alone on a pier in a strange city thinking I may have just witnessed a homicide. Was my life ever going to go back to being simple and uncomplicated?

And was that really a person I saw falling out of one of the cruise ship's portholes? Being *pushed* out of one of the cruise ship's portholes? I waved my hands high in the air on the off chance that someone from the ship could see me so I could tell them what had just happened. There was no way anyone could have spotted anything from the upper decks since the balconies hid the view of the lower row of portholes.

But the only person who saw me from the ship was the man left in the porthole opening. It was too far for me to make out what he looked like except that he was bald and that he was watching me through binoculars.

"Oh no." Turning quickly, I hid my face and ran to the safety of the aisle between the booths so the man with the binoculars couldn't make out who I was. But I ran straight into Cori, Rayelle, and her mom.

"We heard you scream!" Rayelle said.

"What's going on?" Cori was suddenly on high alert. "Did someone try to grab your wallet? Where is he? I'll rearrange his face!"

"No, it's nothing like that. I think—" But I wasn't quite sure what to say. Cori was used to my crazy-sounding stories about killer mers and mortal peril, but I'd just met Rayelle. And maybe I hadn't exactly seen what I thought I'd seen. Maybe the cruise-ship people were just dumping something in the water, like garbage or leftover food. Not like that would be a good thing either, but at least it wasn't a suspected homicide.

But before I could think of how to phrase what I thought I saw, Dillon arrived with an officer in an official-looking uniform. "I'm telling you, man," Dillon said. "I know what I saw."

We all followed Dillon and the officer back onto the pier, but by then the cruise ship had passed. We could only see the stern with the name "Wonderment Cruiselines" as the ship continued into the harbor to dock at the pier by the bridge.

"And I'm telling *you,* if this is another one of your stunts, I'm going to have to ban you from the Straw Market again," the officer replied. He had a name tag with the name "Ensel." I wasn't sure if he was a cop or a security guard. I couldn't see a revolver, yet he could have one hidden somewhere. He had a club attached to his belt, plus a set of handcuffs, so that seemed legit enough. "I swear, Dillon. First I hear you're hassling those necklace kids and now this. Your days here are numbered."

"But listen, man. This girl here saw it too." Dillon turned to me.

"Hi." I lifted my hand in a feeble wave. Now I felt even more unsure of what I'd seen. If this guy Dillon was the troublemaker the officer made him out to be, maybe it was all a huge misunderstanding. Given the past couple months of my life, I wasn't surprised I'd jumped to the worst possible conclusion. But yet, Dillon seemed so convinced.

Officer Ensel took out a notebook and pen and started scribbling in his notebook. "And you are?"

"I'm Jade. Jade Baxter." Should I really be giving out my personal information to someone I just met? Was he really a police officer or some kind of security guard? Maybe I should text Dad to leave his umbrella drink and come over from Señor Frog's. But, urg, my cell phone didn't work here. "I'm not really from around here so I don't know how things like this work."

"Just tell him what you saw," Dillon insisted.

"Well..." I looked from Dillon to Cori and then to Rayelle. "I think I saw a guy throw something out of one of the portholes of that ship out there." I waved my hand toward the disappearing cruise liner.

"It was a body. She saw a body just like me," Dillon added.

"Can you confirm you saw an actual body being dumped into the harbor?" Officer Ensel looked at me with an intense glare. "Could you describe the victim's hair color or approximate height?" I could tell by his tone that he didn't particularly consider Dillon a reliable witness, and as far as he was concerned, this was just another annoyance in his already frazzled day.

"Well, I'm not exactly sure..." If I was just imagining things, which was highly possible, I shouldn't really make a federal case over what just happened. Considering the secrets I had to hide, it was probably best to be vague and let the officer do what he had to do. "It was about the size of a body but—"

"See? Just like I've been telling you," Dillon interrupted. "This ain't just me making up stuff."

"Cool it, Dillon." Officer Ensel held up his pen to stop him before scribbling a few more things in his notebook. "I'll report this and see what I can find out," Officer Ensel said to me while Dillon turned away and stood at the edge of the pier, staring off at the cruise ship as it sailed farther into the harbor.

"You ain't gonna do nothing about it just like when I told you about that necklace crew," Dillon said to Officer Ensel. Then he turned to me. "It was a body. Tell him!"

My mind was a muddle. "It was kind of far away."

Had I thought it was a body because Dillon had *said* it was a body? I wasn't sure if I could really trust what I saw.

Officer Ensel wrote my mom's and dad's names in his notebook along with our hotel information.

"We'll call if we have any more questions," the officer said before disappearing through the aisle back into the Straw Market.

"This is so jacked up." Dillon folded up his lawn chair with a snap and started tossing stuff in his backpack then glared at me. "You know what you saw. Are you too much of a princess to do anything about it? Rich girl like you don't want to get her hands dirty to help anyone like me, huh?"

"No, it's not like that. I just—" I was about to go over to him to try and explain when Rayelle's mom caught my arm.

"Don't mind Dillon," Rayelle's mom whispered in my ear. "I've had to report him half a dozen times for causing trouble around the market."

"Like for what?" I asked.

"Stealing food, panhandling," she replied. "I think he got caught pickpocketing once."

"That was a while ago," Rayelle said quietly.

"It doesn't matter," her mom continued. "Boys like Dillon are trouble."

"Come on," Cori added as she took my arm and led me back to the stalls. "Let's get out of here and get a bit more shopping in before Faye gets back from the airport."

A knot of guilt grabbed at my throat. Maybe Rayelle's mom was right and Dillon was a troublemaker, but that didn't keep me from feeling like I should have backed him up more with Officer Ensel. Even though I wasn't so sure what I'd seen, it hadn't been fair to let Dillon hang out to dry and look bad.

But before I could turn around to apologize, Dillon had gathered all his conch shells in the colorful blanket, loaded them into a small, battered green speedboat, and was sailing off into the Caribbean sun.

He never even looked back.

Cori and I exchanged emails with Rayelle and planned to meet her at the beach by our hotel the next afternoon so she could show us the best place to get our hair braided. By the time we found Dad at Señor Frog's, he'd already had three umbrella drinks. Within five minutes of getting him piled into Faye's van, he was snoring like a lumberjack with an actual Mexican frog in his throat. I grabbed a spot beside him so he wouldn't topple over.

"Poppa's been enjoying the island life, eh?" Faye said with a laugh.

"Yeah, it's kind of nice to see him relax. He's had a bit of a rough year," I said as the van traveled through town on our way back to the hotel. Faye was on her last run of the day, and thankfully she was taking the corners at less than warp speed so I could actually see the beautiful palm trees and blue water from the passing ocean side. "We've all had a pretty crazy year so we're down here to get away from it all. As a matter of fact, my dad and mom are getting married here in a few days."

"A tropical wedding!" Faye beamed. "How wonderful!"

"Yeah, if we can get everything organized and find a wedding officiate to marry them by then, that is," I replied. Then I realized I hadn't bought the conch shells, hadn't looked for flowers, and hadn't even found a tropical shirt for Dad.

Sheesh.

"A wedding officiate, huh?" Faye looked up into her rearview mirror and caught my eye.

"Yeah, all our reservations got canceled and we have to rebook everything from scratch," I replied.

"Which wouldn't have happened if Taylor 'n Tyler

hadn't got us kicked out of the Eutopia!" Cori called out from the seat behind me.

"Taylor 'n Tyler? Really?" A girl of about twelve perked up in the backseat.

"I heard Taylor 'n Tyler are doing a secret concert somewhere in Nassau in a few days," Faye said, wiggling her eyebrows as we crossed the bridge to Paradise Island.

"Aha!" Cori exclaimed. "I told you it was them. Those jerks. I don't care if their latest album just went platinum. They're on my hate list."

"I'm sure they're shaking in their very expensive flip-flops," I joked.

"Ha-ha. Hey, isn't that the ship you just saw?" Cori continued, pointing to the ship next to the Disney Cruise liner. The ship had a huge W on the top, and the words "Wonderment Cruiselines" were scrawled across the stern.

"Looks like it," I replied.

"Look at that waterslide!" Cori exclaimed.

The ship had an enclosed waterslide that ran across the deck's railing and over the ocean. Kids zipped through the waterslide's see-through tube, hundreds of feet above the harbor. It made me want to puke just looking at it.

"That looks horrifying," I said.

"That looks *awesome!*" Cori leaned over my lap to get a better look as we reached the other side of the bridge.

Other than the slide, the rest of the ship looked like all the other ships, with its gleaming hull and sparkling pools on the upper deck. Perfectly normal. Nothing to see. It certainly didn't look like the kind of place where someone would be murdered then dumped into the ocean.

Despite how the last year had gone, not every day was supposed to be filled with plots of murder and mayhem.

Cori was right. I really just needed to chill out.

Chapter Five

ONCE WE RETURNED TO the hotel, I got *lots* of time to chill out when I tried to get ice from the ice machine one floor down and got stuck in the elevator on the way back up.

No joke. I was caught in an elevator in a hotel I'd nick-named "the Asylum." Truly a horror flick in the making.

The whole thing just shuddered to a stop with a groan-ing thud, and the lights even flickered to add to the mood. I was alone on the elevator (of course) so I tried using the red phone meant for emergencies but it was dead (naturally). I banged on the elevator door but I guessed I was between floors because no one answered. Honestly, all I needed was a boa constrictor to drop down from the ceiling and my untimely demise would be complete.

Thankfully, I had my cell phone with me since I'd been using it to take pictures. Even though Mom and Dad hadn't gotten me cell-phone service for our trip to the Bahamas, the hotel Wi-Fi was good enough to connect with Cori back in our hotel room via Video Gab.

"Where's that ice?" Cori asked when she answered. "It's boiling in here."

Oh, yeah—did I mention? In addition to the obvious electrical issues, the Asylum was apparently not very fond of air conditioning.

"I'm stuck in the elevator!" I yelled, motioning to the mirrored walls around me to prove my point. It didn't help that the mirrors kept reflecting my image on and on into infinity, adding to the *Twilight Zone*-ish tone of the moment.

"What?" Cori yelled. "Are you okay?"

I could see Dad's beet-red, sunburned face come into view of Cori's screen. "Jade! Where are you?"

"Get me out of here!" Thoughts of my airplane ride over the Atlantic Ocean buzzed through my head. What was worse, I wondered, spiraling downward into a watery grave or plunging to my death in an elevator shaft? "I'm stuck in the elevator and the service phone doesn't work. Can you call the front desk to let them know I'm trapped in here?"

"I'm on it!" Dad yelled.

"You want me to keep you company on the phone?" Cori asked.

"No. Save your battery," I replied. Cori hadn't brought her phone charger. "Hopefully I'll be out of here in a few minutes."

I hung up and leaned against the elevator, sliding down the wall and sitting on the floor, already regretting not staying on the phone with Cori when I had the chance.

Then it occurred to me that if I could Video Gab with Cori via the Internet in the hotel, I could probably connect with Luke back home too.

I found Luke in my contacts list and pressed the Video Gab icon.

Meanwhile I could hear Cori yelling something down the elevator shaft that sounded like "on the brink."

"What?" I yelled back while my phone's screen showed it was still connecting.

Cori yelled again about "squeezing a bra through the door," and I wasn't sure I *wanted* to know what on earth she was talking about.

"I can't hear you!" I looked up to the ceiling and yelled back.

"Can you hear me now?" my phone called out.

"Oh, hello!" I said to the screen as the video feed kept loading. I wasn't sure it was going to connect until I saw Luke's smiling face staring back. Relief flooded through me. At least if I was going to fall to my death, the last image I'd see was of a super-cute mer-boy.

"Hey, how's it going, stranger?" Luke's smile lit up the screen, and his sandy curly hair fell over his hopelessly blue eyes. "I didn't think I'd be hearing from you. What's happening?"

"You'll never believe it but I'm stuck in an elevator so I thought I'd call," I said.

"What?" Luke laughed out loud. "Is this a joke?"

"I wish," I replied.

"So you're stuck in an elevator and hoping I'll come

break you out of there?" I could see him smirking. "Not really my area of expertise. Now if you were stuck in an *underwater* elevator, maybe."

I laughed, remembering our latest underwater adventures.

"Don't worry. My dad's got someone coming to rescue me," I said.

I picked a piece of ice from the ice bucket and popped it in my mouth.

"Are you eating *ice*?" Luke asked with a laugh.

"It has come to this," I replied. "Next thing you know I'll be eating the soles of my flip-flops."

"What's it like down there in your tropical paradise, anyway?" Luke asked.

"Oh, you know—movie stars and moonlit walks on the beach," I replied.

"Save me one of those," Luke said.

"A movie star or a moonlit walk?" I asked.

"Whichever one ends up in a moonlit kiss," he replied.

"Well, that could go either way, I suppose," I teased. "What's happening back in Port Toulouse?"

"Nothing quite as exciting as what you've got going on down there, apparently. Trey and I got a few more leaf-raking jobs, which I hope we'll finish up by the time we catch our plane on Friday." Luke and Trey mowed lawns in the summer, raked leaves in the fall, and shoveled snow in the winter for extra money. "That is if Trey can get his head on straight before then."

"What's up with Trey? Does it have anything to do with

Cori?" I asked. Maybe I could get a straight answer out of Luke because Cori wasn't talking.

"I'm not exactly sure. He's just been playing a lot of video games and eating cereal, which is pretty normal, except he keeps crashing on level one and he's been eating his cereal with a fork. I was thinking of messing with him and putting green food coloring in the milk. I doubt he'd notice."

Another yell sounded from upstairs, this time it was Dad yelling something about "rappelling down the elevator shaft."

"Don't do anything stupid!" I yelled up to the ceiling.

"I was just kidding," Luke said with a laugh.

"Oh, sorry! I wasn't yelling at you. My dad's just having a nervous breakdown. Sounds like Trey's in need of an intervention too. Get the poor boy a spoon at least," I joked.

"That would be the brotherly thing to do, but I'm not sure it would help. Things were pretty tense around here last night before you guys left. Trey texted something to Cori and she took it all wrong," Luke said.

That's when my "friend gene" kicked in.

"Maybe Cori didn't exactly take it all wrong. Maybe Trey *actually* said something stupid," I blurted out.

"What does it matter? It's really between the two of them," Luke said.

"It matters because Cori is my friend!" I yelled louder than I intended.

Cori shouted from up above with a "You too, girl!"

"Maybe we shouldn't talk about it," Luke said quietly.

"Maybe—" I began. But just then, the elevator jerked to a start. "Oh, I think I'm being rescued."

"I'm glad you survived to live another day," Luke joked, but I could tell our conversation had taken a turn for the weird.

"Too bad the ice didn't survive quite as well," I replied, looking down at my bucket of slush.

By the time I got back to our room, Cori was bopping off the walls, wanting to know every last detail of my elevator drama.

"It really wasn't that exciting. I think I was only in there for a grand total of twelve minutes," I replied.

"I was trying to get a drink to you. Could you hear me? Did you see the straw I squeezed through the elevator doors?" Cori asked.

"*That's* what you were trying to do!" I said with a laugh. "I was Video Gabbing with Luke, and it sounded like you were on the 'brink' of something and trying to squeeze your 'bra' through the door."

"*Drink!* And *straw*, not *bra!*" Cori said with a laugh. "And you were talking to Luke? Was Trey there?" A somber look crossed her face so I tried to keep things light.

"No, I think he was eating or something," I replied, trying to figure out how Luke and my conversation had gotten so tense and convoluted. Was Luke that blind to the fact that his brother had been acting like an ignoramus toward Cori? Wasn't Cori supposed to be his girlfriend, not just another one of his skateboarding buddies?

"Oh," Cori said quietly, staring at her phone. Then something must have occurred to her because she sprang to life. "Hey! I wanted to show you something." She pulled up a video on her phone's screen.

"What on earth...?" I put a hand to my mouth. Gnashing teeth! Ripping flesh! The most terrifying thing I'd ever seen! "What *is* that?"

"A shark dive," Cori said cheerily. "They have them here in the Bahamas. We should totally go."

"Are you out of your mind?" I asked. The video showed the leader of the dive feeding the sharks unidentifiable chunks of meat while other divers looked on. The sharks snatched the fish out of the leader's chain-mailed hand. They even had a *Jaws*-like soundtrack to add to the effect. "People actually do this?"

"Yup. Isn't it awesome? I read on the website that it's almost a guarantee that we'd see some because Caribbean reef sharks and tiger sharks are really plentiful in the Bahamas." Cori stared at the screen with a look of amazement on her face.

"I didn't need to know that," I muttered.

"They even give you a video to keep at the end of your dive!" she added.

"I *really* don't see that as a selling feature," I said.

"Oh, look at that guy!" Cori pointed to the screen. Just then, a shark as big as a submarine went straight for one of the cameramen, teeth gleaming, then zoomed off in the other direction at the last possible second.

"Turn it off. Turn it off!" I waved a hand across my face to try to un-see what I'd just seen.

"Honestly, Jade. As a mermaid, you would think you'd want to work on your shark skills." Cori scowled as she hit Pause on the video. "Don't you want to do anything fun while we're here?"

"If by 'fun' you mean putting my life in mortal peril, then no," I replied, but I could tell Cori was bummed by my reaction. "Also, um. You'll waste all your phone battery downloading videos like that."

A light tap sounded on the door joining our room with Mom and Dad's.

"Okay, I think I finally got your dad settled," Mom said as she entered our room.

Dad's three umbrella drinks and the drama of my elevator rescue must have done him in because Mom had tucked him in to bed. We filled her in on everything that had happened at the Straw Market with Dillon and the cruise ship.

"Well, between that and the elevator, you've certainly had an eventful afternoon!" Mom said. "But it sounds like this Dillon boy is pretty convinced something is going on."

"Rayelle's mom says he's constantly causing trouble around the market," Cori chimed in. "Her mother caught him stealing once, and he was kicked out of the market for six months. He's on probation for now but it looks like he's up to his old tricks again."

"Yes, but we all know how people can be quick to judge," Mom said.

It made me think of the ladies back at Dooley's Drugstore and how they'd said those things about Mom and Dad. I hadn't told Mom about those ladies because I didn't want to upset her. Nothing should ruin their happy day. We'd worked so hard to get to where we were, having our family all back together. It was going to be amazing, going back to Port Toulouse after Mom and Dad made their marriage official, no matter what the rumor mill had to say.

"Jade," Mom continued, "do you think there's something to this boy Dillon's story?"

"Maybe. I'm not saying it was an actual body, though," I replied. "Officer Ensel is right—it's probably nothing. He said they'd call if they needed to ask more questions."

"Did you at least manage to get a look around the market?" Mom asked.

"Yeah, but I didn't get any stuff for the wedding, so the whole trip was a bit of a bust," I said. "How did you do with the planning here?"

"Well," Mom said with a sigh. "The Alyssum already has five weddings booked for Saturday and Sunday so the only thing they can do is get us in for a sunset ceremony at the gazebo on the beach for Saturday evening."

"Oh, that'll be pretty," Cori said.

"They don't have any staff to help, though, so the actual planning is up to us," Mom said, shuffling through the pile of papers and brochures she'd accumulated, trying to sort out the wedding reservations.

"When is everyone arriving?" I asked.

"Eddie and Bobbie are sailing down from Florida on her sailboat and should arrive on Thursday or Friday," Mom said. Eddie was Luke and Trey's grandfather and apparently had made a bit of a love connection with Bobbie over the many hours of video chat they'd had while trying to come up with designs for a mer-to-human synthesizer, which Dad called the Merlin 3001. Bobbie lived in Florida and she had helped Luke turn into a mer-guy for the first time since he was a baby that past spring.

"My parents and the Martins are flying in on Friday," Cori added.

"So everything needs to get organized in the next five days?" I asked, picking up a brochure for wedding cakes.

"It's going to be tight but honestly, I don't want this to take over our whole week," Mom said with a smile. "Hopefully we can enjoy a bit of our vacation in the meantime."

"Can we go Snuba diving?" Cori asked, leafing through a few of the flyers she'd nabbed in the lobby. "Oh, and paragliding. And, oh right! We can swim with sharks!"

"Gah! Not the sharks again," I said with a laugh.

"Yes—let's do it all," Mom said, stroking Cori's hair. We're on vacation, after all. Let's have as much fun as possible and keep our time in the Bahamas as drama-free as possible."

Thinking about what had just happened at the Straw

Market and how much I'd let my imagination run wild, I had to agree.

"Drama-free," I repeated. "Sounds like a great idea to me."

Chapter Six

"THIS IS PROBABLY THE worst idea in the history of bad ideas," I whispered to Cori on Tuesday morning as we got ready for our Snuba-diving excursion off the coast of Paradise Island. I'd convinced her to put off shark diving for a few days (hopefully *forever*), but there was no way Cori was going to leave the island before we at least went Snuba diving.

I wriggled my way into a damp, rubbery wet suit and cursed the makers of neoprene with every fiber of my being. It didn't help that my stomach was grumbling. The boat had left bright and early, so I'd only had time to scarf down a bowl of cereal and a banana since the rest of the hotel's breakfast buffet wasn't supposed to be served for another hour. Talk about a letdown!

Mom and Dad had tagged along, and about a half a dozen other tourists crammed the boat, getting ready for our underwater adventure.

"You're just saying that because you got to spend all summer underwater while I was stuck in *The Lady Sea*

Dragon with Mr. Romance," Cori said as she tucked her dark curls under the strap of her face mask. Cori and Trey had been squabbling ever since the Fall Folly dance when he was supposed to be our date but spent most of his time at the snack table with his buddies. It didn't help once Cori found out Trey hadn't actually ordered the corsages our friend Reese had brought to the dance, even though Trey had jokingly taken credit for them. Things sounded like they had sort of gone downhill from there.

I remembered my conversation with Luke and how I'd practically jumped down his throat defending Cori. Didn't he realize his brother was being a lamebrain? Guys could be so dense sometimes.

"So what's happening with you and Trey anyway? Is it going to be weird when he and Luke get here?" I wasn't sure if Cori and Trey were still actually dating by the time we left on our trip, but Cori was getting fed up with Trey's total lack of a romance in the boyfriend department. It might be awkward for me to be dating Luke if Cori broke up with his brother. We all had so much fun together.

"I dunno. We kind of had a fight before I left, so it's been weird." Cori looked sad for a moment, but then her face brightened in a kind of fake-happy way. "But I don't want to think about that. Come on, Jade. This is my chance to see what you've been seeing all this time. I bet it'll be amazing."

"Believe me, being underwater all summer was anything but amazing. Don't you remember that crazy Dame Council who turned out to be my own grandmother?" I whispered.

"Don't worry. Nobody's trying to rip your arms off around here," Cori replied. She fiddled with the strap on one of her flippers. "Besides, you already know more about this equipment than I do after all that underwater hockey stuff you've been doing."

"Sure, I know how to use a snorkel and mask, but I've never scuba-dived before," I said.

"It's *Snuba* diving, not scuba diving. Much easier and completely safe because all of us are attached to a breathing tube connected to that air tank over there," Cori insisted, pointing to the huge tank of air floating on the water above where we were about to dive. "Totally idiot-proof."

"Idiot-proof is good, I guess. What do you think, Mom?" I asked as I put on my flippers. A few breaths of water instead of air were all it took to switch our "mer" gene on and then it was Tail City. Salt water made the change even quicker, but I'd even transformed into a mermaid in the Port Toulouse community pool a few weeks before, so all these water sports were making me a bit nervous. "This hardly seems like a sane choice for people from our particular culture."

"It'll be fine," Mom whispered to me, looking gung ho. "We'll only be a couple dozen feet underwater, so we can always hold our breath and swim to the surface if anything happens. I'm really looking forward to seeing the ocean in this part of the world."

I could tell Mom was totally into it. I guess if you were a full-fledged mermaid like Mom, seeing a part of the ocean you hadn't even known existed could be fairly interesting. In fact, most mers never got a chance to swim outside the habitat where they grew up. The mers off the coast of Port Toulouse didn't even know that other mers existed beyond their pod.

"Okay, if you say so," I said with a sigh. If Mom thought Snuba diving was okay, I guess it was okay. I switched to my mer voice so only she would hear. *But if we sprout tails, we'll have to get Dad in a bathing suit for your wedding and I can't see that ending well.*

Mom smiled at me while the Snuba instructors helped us with the rest of our equipment, and soon we were all set to go.

"You ladies be careful!" Dad said. His hearing was better but he didn't want to risk making it worse with Snuba diving because of his swimmer's ear. He sat on the boat's deck in shorts, socks, and sandals, with his pasty white legs making him look exactly like the tourist he was.

"You be careful too!" I yelled before putting on my mask and jumping into the water. "And put on some sunscreen!"

As we splashed into the Caribbean waters, our Snuba leader gave us last-minute instructions, repeating some of the highlights from our on-land lesson earlier. Then soon we were all underwater, our hair swaying all around us as we dove and swam, taking in the gorgeous coral, colorful tropical fish, and sea life off the coast of Paradise Island.

This is amazing, Mom rang to me in her mer voice. *It's even more beautiful than I imagined.*

A few tourists from our group looked around the water

when Mom spoke, trying to find the source of the ringing noise, but to them, the high-pitched ring of our mer voices probably sounded like a passing Jet Ski or speedboat. We mers had the added bonus of emitting a frequency that jammed boats' sonar and radar signals so we were invisible on depth sounders and fish finders.

It's so different than the water back home, isn't it? I rang back. The colorful fish and sparkling blue waters of the Bahamas were completely different from the mackerel, lobster, and bottle-green waters off the coast of Port Toulouse. Plus, the Caribbean water was warm and soothing, not freezing cold like in the North Atlantic.

Hey, Mom. How many other pods of mers are there around the world? I rang.

Who knows? Mom replied. *I always thought it was just us back in Port Toulouse. It's not like we have the Internet and television to share that kind of information.*

What about the ocean where Mr. Chamberlain was from, I wondered. How many mers lived there? Or the mers near Bobbie off the coast of Florida? Swimming with my Snuba hose connected to the tank floating above us—as a human underwater—made me marvel at how amazing it was that there were mers in other places in the world, living their aquatic lives without the leash of a Snuba tube.

All I know is that swimming underwater is much more enjoyable when you're not being chased by homicidal merdudes, I joked.

Just as I thought the thought, I saw a flicker out of the

corner of my eye. My heart rose to my throat as I imagined the worst, images of Cori's shark video flashing through my mind.

What was that? I rang to Mom. Were we all about to become shark bait?

Just another diver. Looks like we're not the only ones enjoying the sights today, Mom replied.

Off in the distance, a couple hundred feet away from our group, I could make out the outline of what looked like an actual scuba diver. He (or she) had long flippers and swam through the water with green air tanks on his back. My heart settled back in my chest, safe in the knowledge that I wouldn't get gnashed up into mermaid sushi after all. At least for now.

Maybe we can get Dad to try scuba diving back in Port Toulouse once his ears clear up, Mom said. *Then he could visit our mer-friends back at the village. I bet he'd get a kick out of it.*

That, I'd like to see, I rang with a laugh.

Cori swam a dozen feet or so in front of us. She turned to show us a conch shell she'd found that was like the kind Dillon sold at the Straw Market. A cloud of sand rose from where she'd picked the shell from the ocean floor. I wished I could communicate with her in my mer voice like I was doing with Mom, but I nodded enthusiastically and gave her a thumbs-up.

Cori picked up another shell and handed it to me, but the Snuba instructor motioned for us to leave them because tourists weren't supposed to scavenge anything they saw on underwater dives.

Maybe I'd have to make another trip to Dillon's Treasures after all—if Dillon would even sell shells to me after what had happened. Was Dillon right? I knew I wasn't some spoiled, rich princess, but had I left him high and dry with Officer Ensel because I didn't want to "get my hands dirty"?

One thing was for sure—Snuba diving was awesome. It was so peaceful and amazing with the beautiful, colorful fish darting in and out of swaying seaweed and corals. We didn't see any dolphins (or sharks!) but there were plenty of fish to keep us entertained. We even saw an orange, white, and black "Nemo" fish, which Cori wanted to take home too.

By the time we got back onto the tour boat, we were exhausted but happy.

"So, it was a success?" Dad asked as we pulled off our gear and got ready to return to the island.

"Yeah, it was much more fun than I expected," I replied. "Plus, Mom and I decided we're signing you up for scuba lessons."

"Speaking of which, where did that other scuba diver go?" Mom asked, looking around for another boat.

"Scuba diver? A cruise ship passed earlier but I haven't seen anything else the whole time we've been out here," Dad said.

The captain started up the boat and soon we were heading back to the hotel.

That's strange, Mom rang.

I shrugged, not really giving it a second thought.

Honestly, Snuba diving had worked up a bit of an appetite, and cereal and a banana just weren't cutting it anymore. The main thing on my mind just then was the mile-long buffet table waiting for me back at the Asylum.

Nom. Nom.

Chapter Seven

A FTER PIGGING OUT AT lunch, followed by all the desserts I could possibly pile onto my plate at the Asylum's buffet, I conked out for a nap on a lounge chair under a huge umbrella next to the pool while Cori caught up on all the "Boyfriend or Bust?" and "Crush or Crushed?" relationship quizzes in her teen magazines.

Mom decided to stay back in the room with Dad because he had layered a Snuba boat-ride sunburn over his Señor Frog's sunburn and she wanted to keep an eye on him.

Honestly, I wasn't sure how Dad had managed without Mom for the past year. Since she got back home from the ocean, he'd managed to need six stitches in his hand after an unfortunate encounter with the recycling bin, gone partially deaf from swimmer's ear, gotten tipsy on fancy umbrella drinks at the local Bahamian watering hole, and possibly given himself sunstroke. All in all, though, I had a feeling Dad didn't mind all the attention.

A couple of rowdy college frat boys splashed me awake from my drool nap an hour or so later, just in time for Cori and me to meet Rayelle in front of the hotel to get our hair braided.

"My mom said we have exactly one hour to get our hair done or else she's calling Officer Ensel," I said to Rayelle when Faye dropped her off in front of the hotel. Faye tooted her horn and sped off to her next pickup. Mom was still a bit nervous about letting Cori and me roam around on our own, so it helped to know that Rayelle was with us.

"No problem," Rayelle said. "I texted my cousin, and she's going to meet us on the beach below the Eutopia Resort where she usually braids hair."

"Well, if we can't *stay* at the Eutopia, at least we can get their braids," Cori joked.

"Are you still bitter about Taylor 'n Tyler possibly bumping our reservation?" I asked.

"Possibly?" Cori retorted. "I swear if I see Taylor 'n Tyler anywhere, I'm going to give them and their sappy love songs a piece of my mind."

I had a feeling Cori took more offense at Taylor 'n Tyler's sappy love songs than the idea that they'd bumped our reservation. She'd once told me Taylor 'n Tyler's song "Make Me Wanna Fly" was playing on the outdoor speakers at the skate park the first time she went there with Trey, and she played that song over and over whenever she came to my house.

We cut through the outdoor pool area of the Asylum, past the college boys splashing each other at the swim-up bar, and took the stairs down onto the beach. The crystal blue Caribbean Sea glittered in the afternoon sun, and the white sand squished between our toes as we chatted the whole way along the half-mile stretch of beach from the Asylum to the Eutopia. We walked along the shoreline, splashing our feet through the water.

"Hey there, Kiki," Rayelle said once we met up with a pretty girl in her early twenties who wore a colorful, flowered wrap dress, her hair in super-long, black corn-row braids that were beaded at the bottoms. The beads clinked together musically as she turned to greet us.

"My favorite customer," Rayelle's cousin said in a sing-song voice.

"Cori, Jade, this is my cousin Kiki," Rayelle said, turning to us.

"You girls ready to get some braids in that pretty hair of yours?" Kiki asked with a toothy white smile.

We all chatted about what type of style we wanted. Cori decided to get the whole front of her hair done, leaving the back of her hair unbraided. I opted for just a few braids off to one side. Kiki got started on Cori first.

We talked about the weather, the resort, and the local gossip while Kiki fashioned braid after braid in Cori's hair.

"You're really amazing at this," I said, marveling at how quickly Kiki's creation was taking shape.

"Lots of practice," Kiki said with a hearty laugh. "Rayelle used to help me, but where you been, girl?" Kiki asked as her fingers worked nimbly through Cori's hair. "I ain't seen you since this summer."

"Ah, you know. Helping Mama at the market. Plus school and everything," Rayelle said.

"Those kids still hassling you?" Kiki asked.

Rayelle pursed her lips and gave Kiki a look, shaking her head as though she wanted Kiki to drop it. I wondered what Kiki's comment was all about, but Rayelle was beginning to look a little uncomfortable.

"So…" I began, trying to change the subject, "that got a little crazy back at the Straw Market yesterday, huh?"

"You mean with Dillon? Yeah, I wanted to tell him I saw Officer Ensel talking to a Wonderment Cruiselines guy later yesterday but I haven't seen him since," Rayelle replied.

"How'd you know the guy was from Wonderment Cruiselines?" I asked.

"He had this hat with the ship's big W crest on it," Rayelle said.

"Well, that should make Dillon feel better," I said. At least it sounded like Officer Ensel was taking him seriously.

"Yeah, if I could find him to tell him," Rayelle said.

"Is Dillon still spewing his nonsense?" Kiki asked as she slid a bead expertly along one of Cori's braids. "Nothing but trouble, that boy."

"He's not that bad," Rayelle said quietly, as if trying to wrap up the conversation. That was interesting. Hadn't Rayelle's mom said what a troublemaker Dillon was? Why was Rayelle defending him?

"Not that bad?" Kiki said as she wound a thin elastic band around the end of one of Cori's braids. "You should have been here last night. He came to pick up my boy-friend, Johnny, with that green speedboat of his. Johnny said Dillon was trying to get him to sneak onto one of the cruise ships at the shipyard, but Johnny told him he had to get back to work."

"Which cruise ship?" I asked as Kiki motioned for me to take Cori's place so she could get started on my braids while Cori examined her hair masterpiece in a hand mirror.

"Not sure," Kiki replied. "Whichever it was, I'm sure that boy is up to no good."

I thought about that for a second while I sorted through the tray of beads Kiki handed to me, trying to decide which color to choose. Could it be Wonderment Cruiselines? I'd been trying to put it out of my mind, but Dillon seemed to still be convinced that something strange was going on aboard that ship.

"That's them!" Cori put down the hand mirror and grabbed her bag, searching for her phone.

"Who?" I tried to turn to see who she was talking about but Kiki held my hair tightly as she braided it.

"Taylor 'n Tyler!" Cori exclaimed. "Those are the guys who got us kicked out of the Eutopia. I'm gonna get proof once and for all."

Out of the corner of my eye, I saw Cori jog down the beach to meet up with a bleached-blond, tanned couple surrounded by several bodyguards.

"Hey! Taylor 'n Tyler," Cori called out. She took out her phone and held it up to record the conversation. "Did you know you guys bumped our reservation at the Eutopia and ruined a whole wedding? I thought your songs were all about love and romance. Well, you're nothing but a couple of romance crushers!"

Looking surprised, Taylor Ariella looked over to where Cori was standing. She leaned over to Tyler Green and said, "What's that girl talking about?"

Tyler shrugged and was about to say something, but before he could reply, a beefy-looking security guard with a black T-shirt and dark sunglasses snatched Cori's phone out of her hand and threw it into the sand. He and his no-neck buddies took Taylor 'n Tyler by the arm and shuttled them back up the stairs leading to the Eutopia Resort.

"Hey! Not cool!" I called out to the security guards and leaped from my chair, leaving a chunk of my hair behind in the process. I ran to Cori's side, Kiki calling after me that she hadn't finished my braid. I found Cori's phone in the sand and shook it off before handing it back to her. "Are you okay?"

"Yeah, I'm fine but can you believe those guys?" Cori was about to run after them when I caught her arm.

"Forget about them," I said.

"Yeah, they're not worth it," Rayelle agreed, joining us. "They're just a couple of hotshots who think they can get away with that kind of thing. Some people just think they're untouchable."

I studied Rayelle, wondering if she was talking about Taylor 'n Tyler or something else.

Cori watched as Taylor 'n Tyler's group disappeared into the Eutopia Resort. "Those guys haven't heard the last of me," she vowed.

"If you don't watch out, you're going to end up in one of those celebrity magazines you love so much," I teased. "Let's just finish getting our hair braided, get some snacks, and then go chill by the pool. I promise I won't even fall asleep this time."

"All right, all right," Cori said, tossing her beaded, braided hair over her shoulder so the beads clinked together like Kiki's. "But this hair is making me feel fierce so those guys better watch their step."

Faye picked up Rayelle on her next run to the airport so Rayelle could help at her mom's stall, and Cori and I headed back up to our room. We knocked on the adjoining door to Mom and Dad's room, and Dad came out with his shiny, sunburned face smelling like aloe vera.

"Nice braids!" Mom said as she followed Dad into our room.

"Yeah," Dad agreed. His ears had finally cleared so he didn't have to yell everything. "Micci, you should get yours done too."

"I need a hair intervention but I don't think braids would help." My mom's hair had grown an inch or two since she'd cropped it short and dyed it blond to go incognito as Tanti Natasha, but it wasn't quite long enough to braid. "I really should have had it done before our trip but there was no time."

"There's a salon downstairs near the main lobby," Cori suggested. "It didn't look too busy. Maybe they can fit you in."

"Yeah, Micci," Dad agreed. He got a sly look on his face and I could tell he was up to something. "Why don't you go downstairs and see if you can get an appointment, and I'll hang with the girls by the pool?"

"Are you sure?" Mom asked, sweeping her bangs away from her face.

"Definitely," Dad said.

"We just need to make sure we have enough time to go into town to get our marriage license now that we've been on the island for twenty-four hours," Mom reminded him.

"Don't worry. I checked the website and we'll have lots of time," Dad said.

We all traveled down in the elevator together, and Mom headed down the hallway off the lobby where there were a few souvenir shops, a convenience store, and the hair salon. Dad made a beeline for the hotel's front desk and soon was deep in conversation with the concierge and poring over several brochures. We sat on one of the plush velour sofas by the entry.

"So much for hanging by the pool," I said to Cori after we'd been sitting there for what seemed like an eternity.

But it didn't look like Cori was listening. She had her phone out and seemed to be checking her email on the hotel's Wi-Fi.

"Anything happening back home?" I asked. Considering the last conversation I'd had with Luke, I wasn't sure if Cori and Trey were actually talking to each other.

"Nah," Cori replied. "It doesn't matter anyway. *Urban Teen* already told me my love life was 'WTH?' and *Teen Reality* only gave Trey and me a four out of ten on their 'Romancerator.'"

"Are you seriously taking relationship advice from a magazine with a 'Romancerator'?" I teased.

Cori shrugged and sighed.

"Hey, wanna go check out the convenience store?" I asked. "I'm starving."

Sure, the buffets at the Asylum were okay, but I didn't really function well on scheduled breakfasts, lunches, and dinners. Didn't anyone in the Bahamas ever hear of the mid afternoon munchies? Late-night snack attacks?

"Sounds like a plan," Cori said, tossing her phone back in her bag.

We waved to Dad to signal we were heading to the convenience store and he waved back to go ahead, that he'd only be a few more minutes, so we headed down the hallway. I could see that Mom was being seated in a salon chair across the hall so it looked like she was going to be there for a while. Whatever plan Dad was cooking up, it seemed to be working.

"I wonder if they have Oreos," I said as we browsed through the aisles once we arrived at the store.

"Oh, snacks! Great idea." Dad arrived moments later with a silly grin plastered on his face. "Make sure to get corn chips too, Jade."

"I bet they have all the snacks you can eat at the Eutopia," Cori muttered.

"Ah, Cori. I'm sorry I messed up our reservation there." Dad gave Cori an understanding smile. "Your dad told me how much you were looking forward to it."

"It's okay. It's just…" Cori said. I could tell her eyes were welling up, and I had a feeling it had something to do with Trey, but I didn't want to embarrass her in front of Dad.

"Cori was just looking forward to the waterslides," I chimed in as I sorted through a rack of vacation T-shirts and held one with a "So Over It" logo up to my chest.

Cori perked up. "Oh, right! The waterslides at the Eutopia are supposed to be amazing. There's this one where you go through a tunnel right through a *shark* tank."

"Again with the sharks?" I muttered. Why, why, *why* did I have to mention the waterslides? I kept sorting through the rack of funny T-shirts and willed myself to keep my mouth shut before Dad and Cori planned any more death-defying activities.

"Is that something you girls would like to do?" Dad asked.

"Totally!" Cori exclaimed.

Too late.

"Well, if that's the case, you two are going to like the surprise I have planned for tomorrow," Dad said, his eyes gleaming. "I just booked a catamaran ride for Micci and me as a wedding present, and I was thinking I could get you guys day passes to the Eutopia Teen Club."

"Teen Club?" I asked, looking up from a "Life's a Beach" T-shirt. I was pretty sure that whatever "Teen Club" was, it was going to be lame.

"Oh, I saw that on their website!" Cori said.

I was about to say that *actual* teens wouldn't be caught dead in a place called Teen Club, but Cori looked so darn happy, and I really wanted her to have a good time this trip no matter what was going on back home, so I decided to keep my trap shut.

"I'm told you can use all the facilities, including the waterslides, so you're sure to get your fix," Dad said.

"And we can pet the stingrays and swim with the dolphins, and oh! Maybe we can do that aquarium dive, Jade," Cori said. Honestly, I wondered if I should keep reminding Cori I was an aqua-phobic mermaid because that fact didn't seem to be on her radar at all this trip.

"Great, then," Dad replied. "It's settled."

"Yeah, great." I tried to agree with as much enthusiasm as I could muster. Mom and Dad deserved a nice day together during their wedding slash honeymoon trip. If I had to suffer a day in something called "Teen Club," I guess I could suck it up.

"Oh, and perfect—Oreos." I snatched the pack of cookies before heading to the cash register.

Might as well carbo-load before our big day sliding through shark-infested waters.

C ORI AND I DID end up chilling out by the pool that Tuesday afternoon, but the Oreos were stale and the frat boys were still up to their shenanigans. But something had been nagging at me about the cruise-ship business ever since Kiki told us about Dillon and her boyfriend earlier on the beach.

Was Dillon trying to sneak onto that cruise ship? Was he on some kind of vigilante mission because no one believed him? I really needed to check things out before we got stuck in Teen Club the next day because even though Dillon had been kind of a jerk, calling me a "rich princess," if he did something stupid, I was afraid I'd feel guilty for not backing him up for the rest of our vacation.

The fact that Mom and Dad still needed to go into town for their marriage license was a convenient excuse for me to casually suggest we could drop in at the Straw Market too.

"And how are the plans going for the happy couple?" Faye asked as Cori, Dad, Mom, and I rode in her shuttle van on our way back to town. It was already Tuesday and the wedding was supposed to be in four days, but the only thing Mom and Dad had managed to rebook was the beachside gazebo at the Asylum.

"I called the town just before we left, and they said they couldn't guarantee an officiate because of all the weddings happening this weekend." Mom pulled off her sunglasses and pinched the bridge of her nose. "If I can't find someone to marry us before Saturday, I'm afraid we're going to have to cancel the whole thing. In front of all our guests, urg…"

"Don't worry, Micci," Dad said. "I'm sure it will all work out."

But it wasn't fair that after all this time, their plans kept getting messed up just because our reservation at the Eutopia got bumped. I was beginning to feel the same growing rage Cori had for Taylor 'n Tyler for wrecking everything.

"I hope so," Mom replied.

"Now, don't worry. It ain't over till it's over," Faye replied, grinning at us in her rearview mirror. "Tell you what. Town Hall isn't very far from the Straw Market. Why don't I drop you two off there to see if you can sort things out, and Rayelle can hang out with the girls at the market until you're done?"

Mom didn't seem convinced. "I don't know. Are you sure you girls will be okay?"

"Don't worry, Mrs. Baxter," Faye said. "My grand-daughter Rayelle is very responsible—plus her mama is there if they need anything."

"We won't be able to get into too much trouble with Rayelle there. She is stricter than three moms and a grade-school principal," Cori said.

"I can vouch for that," Dad said.

"Well, okay, if you're sure," Mom said.

By then we were downtown. Faye slowed the van to let Mom and Dad out in front of Town Hall and texted Rayelle to tell her we were coming.

"Rayelle says she is on her way to meet them now," Faye said, putting down her phone.

"Thank you, Faye." Mom put her sunglasses back on before looking back to Cori and me in the backseat. "You two be good, and we'll meet you at the market in about an hour."

Faye continued onward to the Straw Market, and we said our good-byes when she let us out at the top of the lane where we met up with Rayelle.

For a late Tuesday afternoon, things were bustling in the Straw Market. I veered around the group with the shell necklaces, remembering what Rayelle had told us about them last time. The same girl who had tried to sell me a necklace bumped Rayelle in the shoulder as she brushed by.

"Hey!" Cori yelled. But I caught her arm before she went all postal on the girl.

"Forget about her," Rayelle said. "Let's just go."

We walked a bit more, past Señor Frog's and a few of the outside booths.

"What's her problem, anyway?" I asked, looking back at the girl as she hid her mouth with her hand and said something to one of her friends and laughed.

"She's just part of a group at school that likes to make my life hell," Rayelle said. "They pick on me 'cause I'm tall, or they pick on me 'cause I get good grades. They really don't need a reason—they're just jerks."

"Well, if that's all they can find wrong with you, I guess they have more of a problem than you do," Cori said.

"Yeah, I guess," Rayelle said. "It just got really bad at the end of last year. That was when Dillon was still in school and he had my back."

Aha. So that's why Rayelle didn't chime in when her mom was trash-talking Dillon. I wondered if Rayelle's mom knew Dillon was actually looking out for her.

"So why isn't Dillon in school now?" I asked.

"He's sixteen and his mom wants him to work more. There's a lot going on at home," Rayelle said, walking ahead as if wanting to put an end to the conversation. "Let me just tell my mom I'm going to hang out with you guys, and I'll come find you in a sec."

Fair enough. Not like it was any of my business.

"Hey, isn't that Officer Ensel?" I asked Cori when I spotted a man in a familiar dark blue uniform on the stairs of a nearby building. I really wanted to go ask him if there were any new leads on the Wonderment Cruiselines case, but he was busy texting someone on his phone, and by the serious look on his face, it looked important.

"Who? The police officer? Didn't you say you were going to forget about all that stuff?" Cori whispered as we walked past him. "No drama, remember?"

Even if I couldn't get to talk to him, I was glad Officer Ensel was investigating the situation. Maybe it would make Dillon feel better.

"Yeah, you're right. We need to get ready for this wedding! Let's go look at the conches first," I suggested. That way, I could give Dillon the heads-up.

"Way to let it go." Cori glanced at me with a knowing look and laughed.

We wove our way through the stalls until we got to the harbor side of the market, but there was no sign of Dillon or his colorful blanket full of shells. I walked up and down the pier, looking for his green beat-up speedboat, but the only boats there were a few water taxis.

"Wasn't this where he was yesterday?" Cori asked.

"He was right by that entry we just came through." I pointed back to the lane where we'd exited. "I don't see his boat anywhere."

"So that's that, then?" Cori asked.

"I guess so," I said softly as we turned back for the Straw Market stalls.

That *was* that—I'd done what I could. I tried to find Dillon to tell him not to worry, that Officer Ensel was on the case. I'd even intended to apologize for not backing him up but Dillon had obviously moved on.

With my conscience semi-clear, I guess it was time for me to move on too.

After not finding Dillon anywhere, we explored the market until we connected with Mom and Dad. We continued shopping while Rayelle went back to her mother's stall to give her a hand.

"How'd it go at Town Hall?" I asked.

Dad produced an official-looking document and beamed. "Marriage license!"

"So you're all set, then?" I asked hopefully.

"They still don't have anyone available to marry us on Saturday," Mom said, looking as disappointed as ever.

"I'm sure everything is going to work out," I said, trying to reassure her, but even I could tell that things were looking grim.

"Let's just work under the assumption that we're still having a wedding on Saturday," Dad said, trying to be encouraging.

"Yeah, all the fun is in the planning anyway, right? And you can't go wrong with the right accessories," Cori added.

Mom smiled and gave us each a kiss. We made a plan to divide and conquer until we found all the things on our list.

Cori found the shell ring for Lainey like she was hoping she would, and we picked out necklaces for the wedding party in the process. I also found a wrap around floral skirt I could wear with a shirt I'd brought with me (thanks to Cori's help). We reconnected with Mom at the end of the market an hour or so later, long enough for my stomach to start grumbling and signal that it was probably time to head back to the Asylum for dinner.

"Did you find a shirt for Dad?" I asked.

"Yup. What do you think?" Dad held a Hawaiian-type shirt up to his chest. He was also sporting a floppy straw hat.

"I think the shirt is perfect, but that hat is going to make you look like even more of a tourist than you already are," I joked.

"Well, I need something to keep him from burning to a crisp," Mom said, kissing Dad on the cheek. "Let's see if we can get a cab back to the hotel, shall we?"

We made it back to Rayelle's mother's booth to see if she could call Faye to pick us up.

"I'm sorry but my grandma just called to say she had to run a really important errand and she won't be able to pick you guys up after all," Rayelle said.

"That's okay," Mom said. "Faye has been wonderful but we can always call another taxi."

"Or I guess there's always the water taxi," I said, remembering the water-taxi driver ready to shuttle tourists anywhere their hearts desired.

"Oh, can we?" Cori asked. She had turned into a bit of a water nut.

Mom smiled and folded Dad's shirt under her arm. "That sounds like a fantastic idea."

We walked back to the edge of the pier. I figured it was only fair to pick the same water-taxi driver who had given me his sales pitch the day before. Turns out his name was Raymond.

We sailed along the island's coast, back toward the channel that led between Nassau and Paradise Island, and passed half a dozen cruise ships docked at the shipyard. The Wonderment Cruiselines ship must have left port already because it was nowhere to be seen. A little farther down the pier, a much smaller boat bobbed in the water, looking like a thimble next to the massive ships.

"Hey, isn't that Dillon's speedboat?" I yelled over the noise of the water taxi's outboard motor. Cori shot me a look, which I ignored.

"Who?" Dad asked.

"That guy who was selling conches yesterday. He's the one I was telling you about." I turned to Raymond. "You know him, right?"

"Yeah, I know Dillon," Raymond said. "He helped me untangle a rope from my propeller once. Dove right in and cut it free. That boy swims like a fish. I'm not sure if that's his boat, though."

I remembered how Rayelle's cousin said Dillon had tried to get her boyfriend to sneak onto the cruise ship the day before. Had Dillon come back to try to do it himself? Rayelle said he hadn't been around the market. Had he been hanging around the shipyard since yesterday?

But the cruise ship was gone.

So, if that was Dillon's boat, where was Dillon?

Chapter Nine

I COULD BARELY GET TO sleep Tuesday night, partly due to the hotel's broken air conditioner, partly due to the balcony's sliding glass door shuddering in its doorframe from the growing wind, and partly due to the college frat-boy party happening next door.

Plus, my mind kept whirling with everything that had happened since we touched down in the Bahamas not even two days before, especially where that guy Dillon was concerned. What if that really was his speedboat at the shipyard? But maybe there was a simple explanation for his boat being there. Maybe (and I'm sure Cori would agree) I should just leave well enough alone.

But when I finally fell asleep, I dreamed Cori and I were standing in a green speedboat bobbing in the middle of the ocean surrounded by dolphins. We both had Wonderment Cruiselines baseball caps on our heads with our beaded braids swinging in the breeze.

"Look! They're all around us!" Cori kept squealing and jumping around in the boat, excited that the dolphins were close enough to touch, but I kept screaming for her to stop freaking out as the boat bobbed wildly in the water, threatening to tip over.

By the time I woke up the next morning to the sound of my cell phone's Video Gab alert, I had a headache that felt like a harpoon had been embedded in my cranium. I pressed the Connect button so Video Gab could load (*if* the hotel paid its Internet bill, that is) but couldn't muster the energy to peel my head off the pillow.

"Hallumph?' I said through squinty eyes, trying to figure out who was calling me so early in the morning.

"Jade?" The image finally loaded and it was Luke, looking bright-eyed and bushy-tailed. And alarmingly cute. There was a lot of background noise so his voice echoed when he spoke, and something that sounded like announcements blared around him, making it hard to hear.

"Luke?" I asked, wiping the drool from the side of my mouth. Charming. "Where are you?"

I looked over to the other bed, expecting to see Cori, but from the sound of the running water in the bathroom, I guessed she was already in the shower getting psyched for our day at Eutopia's Teen Club. The brochure said we could swim with dolphins at Dolphin Lagoon in the afternoon so that's all she'd talked about ever since.

Oh, right. Dolphins. My dream was starting to make a bit more sense.

Luke looked like he was adjusting a few settings on his phone to see and hear more clearly.

"My dad got back from his trip a day early and Mom got someone to cover for her at the flower shop so we got earlier flights," Luke answered brightly. He looked really excited to be heading our way. It was almost as though we hadn't had that weird conversation in the elevator where I pretty much told him his brother was a loser.

"What time is it?" I mumbled, but I could see it was almost 8 a.m. from the clock radio beside my bed. I vaguely remembered Mom popping her head into our room earlier to let me know they were leaving for their catamaran trip and to get up because Teen Club was expecting us by nine. "Are you at the airport or something?"

"Yeah," he replied but I could already see he was sitting in the airport lounge, with other passengers milling around him. "Our flight is supposed to board in about an hour but we're connecting through New York so we won't get to the Bahamas until about three-ish."

It would be Luke's first time flying too. I bet *he* wouldn't need deep breathing techniques just to get through takeoff.

"Too bad you're not here now. Cori and I are going to hang out at something called 'Teen Club.'" I rubbed my eyes and yawned.

"You look so excited by the prospect," Luke said with a laugh.

"Cori's pumped, so I'm sure it'll be fun," I said with as much enthusiasm as I could muster that early in the morning.

"Hey, how's it going?" Trey photo-bombed into the video screen and flashed me a peace sign. All of a sudden I felt like a total jerk for saying those things about him to Luke. Trey really was a good guy. He'd helped us out *so* much that summer, often putting his life on the line to get us through all the mer drama. The guy might be a bit of a goofball, but at least his heart was in the right place.

Speaking of drama, the dream about Dillon's speedboat was still fresh in my mind. Should I clue the guys in to everything that had been happening in the Bahamas since we arrived? No. What was there to tell, really?

"Hey there, Trey. You want to talk to Cori?" I looked over to the bathroom door and tried to listen to hear if the water was still running. "I can get her if you want."

"No," Trey said quickly. "That's okay. Just tell her I said hi." Then he disappeared out of the picture.

"Um, so I guess we'll catch up when we get there?" Luke asked, looking off screen as though he was trying to catch something Trey was saying.

"Yeah. Cool," I replied, getting up to step outside onto the balcony to get some fresh air. If I craned my neck, I could almost see the ocean, reminding me of our water-taxi ride from the night before. "Do you have the address for the new hotel?"

"Actually our reservation at the Eutopia is okay, so we're still staying there," Luke replied. "My mom and dad must have booked it separately from yours."

"Oooo…Cori is *not* going to be too happy about that," I joked. "She's pretty bitter we got bumped."

"Well, what can I say?" Luke said, leaning back and draping his free arm across the back of the bench where he was sitting. "I'm sure they'll have the celebrity suite all ready for us."

"Sorry, dude. Taylor 'n Tyler already beat you to it," I replied. "Anyway, that Teen Club thing is over at the Eutopia, so come find us when you get here." But my mind wasn't on Teen Club just then. I took one last look at the ocean then glanced back at the clock radio and did a bit of mental math.

"Cool. See you then," Luke replied, putting on his sunglasses. "If I don't get mobbed for autographs, that is."

"Get your stuff," I said to Cori as soon as she got out of the shower.

Now that I was wide-awake and could process the dream with the green speedboat, I had to go check things out at the shipyard before I lost my nerve. It reminded me of the time I'd dreamed of floating in the ocean with long strands of silk pulling me underwater—right before I turned into a mermaid for the first time! Not that I thought I was some kind of psychic or anything, but the speedboat dream seriously had me freaked.

"What do you mean, get my stuff? Teen Club doesn't start for another hour. My hair is still soaked," Cori said.

"Just trust me," I said, tossing a few things in my bag. I hustled Cori into mismatched clothes (under much protest), and she peppered me with questions as I rushed her out the door. "You'll see when we get there."

"I *cannot* believe you made me wear this just so you could drag me all the way out here. This tank top was never meant to be seen with these palazzo pants, you know." It would take a long time for Cori to forgive me for that particular fashion trauma but I just couldn't help it. I had to see if the speedboat we saw the night before was Dillon's.

"It's got to be around here somewhere," I said, hunting around until we saw the green speedboat bobbing in the water along the shipyard pier. Thankfully, we'd only had to walk a mile or so from our hotel to get to the shipyard, but we really needed to hustle if we wanted to get back to Teen Club at the Eutopia before nine.

"And so what if it is?" Cori asked.

"I'm telling you, the dream has to mean something. Don't you think it's weird that a speedboat just like Dillon's is abandoned here after he witnesses what he thinks is a murder?" I asked.

"A murder? Seriously, Jade?" Cori shook her head and narrowed her eyes in a look of exasperation.

"Well, okay. Maybe not a murder," I said as I started to climb down onto the boat. "But it's still weird."

"What are you doing?" Cori whispered, shooting furtive looks along the shipyard.

"I have to find out if it's really Dillon's or not," I replied as I stepped onto the boat. It shifted beneath me just like in my dream as I hunted around the gas tank and under a tarp in the bow. Sure enough, there was the colorful blanket Dillon used at the Straw Market. I pulled it back to reveal the seashells tucked away inside. I looked up at Cori and gave her an "I told you so" eyebrow wiggle.

"So fine, it's his boat," Cori replied, glancing at her watch. "But if we're late for Teen Club, they'll be sending Officer Ensel and his SWAT team out for us."

"Okay, I'm coming," I replied. But I was reminded of something when Cori said Officer Ensel's name. Should I call him to tell him about Dillon's abandoned boat? But if Dillon was actually doing something stupid, maybe I should email Rayelle first to see what she thought.

I was about to climb out of the boat when a neon blue string caught my eye. At first, I thought it was part of the tarp, but it came free when I pulled on it.

"What's this?" I asked, holding up the loop of bright blue cord. It was about the length of a necklace and had a metal clip attached to one end.

"Is that a whistle or something?" Cori asked, squinting to see from her vantage point up on the pier. "Maybe it's a boat-safety thing."

"No, this metal part is a clip. Like to attach something. It looks like one of those badge holders my dad gets whenever he goes to engineering conferences. Why would Dillon have one?" I asked.

"Maybe he just got back from a Caribbean conch collector conference or something. Seriously, Jade—who cares? Just hurry!" Cori called down to me. "Someone's coming."

"Hold your horses," I said as I stashed the blue cord under the tarp and scrambled back up to the pier just as two dockworkers turned the corner and headed in our direction.

"Come on before they see us." Cori tugged at my shirt.

"These flip-flops weren't built for speed, you know!" I said, trying to keep up.

"No kidding!" Cori said over her shoulder as she ran ahead in the direction of the Eutopia, as fast as her mismatched palazzo pants could carry her.

Chapter Ten

W E MADE IT TO the Teen Club with only seconds to spare. Emailing Rayelle would have to wait because the rest of the day ended up being a minute-to-minute micromanaged busy-fest with enough activities jammed in to last me a lifetime. Cori seemed to welcome the distractions, though, from the archery to the rock climbing to the Behemoth Shark Waterslide, especially after she found out Luke and Trey were arriving that afternoon.

"Dude," Cori said once we'd finished lunch and were getting ready for our swim with the dolphins at Dolphin Lagoon. "You ready for the main event?"

We walked out onto the gorgeous white-sand beach of the lagoon in our short-sleeved blue wet suits.

"Totally!" I said, giving her a high five. I had to admit that I was kind of looking forward to it too, especially after spending the morning coming nose to teeth with a kajillion sharks through that death-defying Behemoth Shark Waterslide fiasco, confirming *once and for all* that I never, ever, ever wanted to come in contact with a shark again in my life.

Ever.

"It's too bad Luke and Trey are missing out on all the fun, though," I continued.

The look on Cori's face was enough to tell me that I'd just put my flipper in my mouth.

"Ah, what's the matter, Cori?" I asked. "Is it Trey?"

"Yeah, I guess," Cori replied. "I don't think I was ready for the fact that he's coming a day early. I was hoping to have things figured out by now." She looked around at all the swaying palm trees and took a deep breath.

"Are you guys going to be okay?" I asked.

"All I know is that if he can't step it up in the boyfriend department in a place like the Bahamas, we're probably 'Splitting to Splitzville' just like *Totally Teen Talk* magazine predicted."

Just then, the counselors gathered everyone from a few different age groups and broke us up into teams of six for the dolphin swim. Our group included two fifteen-year-olds and a thirteen-year-old girl with her little brother who was super quiet and looked a little shy.

"Okay, everyone. Let's get started," the trainer in the black wet suit said in his lilting Caribbean accent. He looked like he was in his early twenties. "My name is John and I'm a dolphin trainer."

John went through a few rules and regulations before we all got into the water. As soon as I stepped in, an odd sense of familiarity swept over me, which was weird since I'd never been to Dolphin Lagoon before. In fact, I'd never seen a dolphin before.

"There they are," Cori squealed, pointing out a few dolphins playing on the other side of the lagoon.

"Oh, wow." I couldn't help it. The sight of the dolphins' sleek gray bodies and smiling mouths took my breath away. "I never realized how beautiful they'd be."

The dolphins swam around the lagoon in graceful circles, showing off for the crowd with high flips and waving their flippers as they swam past. They were almost human-like in the way they moved and interacted with the crowd.

Our trainer took a few pieces of fish out of his satchel and lured a couple of the dolphins our way.

Fish!

I looked around, trying to figure out if I'd actually heard what I thought I'd heard.

Fish! Fish! Fish!

"Um, Cori?" I tugged her arm, but she was already wading onward, trying to get a chance to pet one of the dolphins.

"Cori!" I said more forcefully through clenched teeth.

"What?" she said, turning to me.

"I think I can understand them." I hid my mouth with my hand so no one could see what I was saying.

"Well, the trainer has a bit of an accent but it's not like he's speaking another language," Cori whispered.

"Not the trainer. The..." I waved my other hand in front of my body like a swimming fish to signal I meant the dolphins. Cori looked at me, confused at first, but then her eyes popped open when she finally clicked on what I meant.

"How can you do that?" Cori asked.

"I don't know. It's like the squeaking they do is on the same frequency as you-know-whats or something," I replied.

"That's just *weird.*" Cori snatched her hand back from one of the dolphins, realizing there was more to them than met the eye. "What are they saying? Are they plotting against us?"

"Mostly they're just excited about the fish, I think," I replied. *Fish! Fish!*

The trainer made a few hand signals to get the show started and the dolphins swam like lightning bolts across the lagoon, turned back, and shot up out of the water into the air in front of us, splashing us all in the process.

"Well, they certainly know how to put on a show." Cori laughed and sputtered water.

"Okay, everyone," John said, handing out small silver fish to each of us while another trainer rounded up the dolphins. "I'm going to give you each a turn to feed a fish to a dolphin."

The fifteen-year-olds, Kylie and Sylvie, went first, tossing a fish in each of the dolphins' mouths.

Fish! Fish! the dolphins squealed.

"Seriously? 'Fish'? Is that all they can say?" I whispered to Cori. "I thought dolphins were supposed to be the ocean's most intelligent creatures."

"No, that would be *you*," Cori said with a wink. "Still, you must admit they're pretty cute."

"They've got that going for them," I agreed.

When it was our turn, Cori just about passed out from excitement.

"I can't believe I'm feeding a dolphin. Oh my god! Jade! Are you watching this?" The dolphin stuck its snout out and pecked her on the cheek. "He's giving me a kiss! That's more romance than I've seen in weeks."

At first, the dolphin wouldn't come near me, but John the trainer managed to coax it to come closer. It was still a bit skittish as it approached, checking me out to see if I could be trusted.

"Just hold the fish up in the air for him to take it," John coached.

I smiled and held out the fish.

Here's your fish, I rang in my mer voice to the dolphin without thinking.

The dolphin must have decided I was okay because it took the fish from me and gobbled it up.

Thanks, dude, the dolphin replied.

I stared at it as it swam away, wondering if I'd heard what I thought I'd heard.

"I really mean it," Cori said as if finishing a sentence.

"*What* do you mean?" I asked.

"I mean thanks for doing this with me," Cori said as she kept feeding fish to the dolphins.

Fish!

"It's, er, not a problem," I replied, giving my head a shake for thinking the dolphin had actually called me "dude."

"Thanks for the whole week, actually," Cori continued. "I really needed to take my mind off things, and you made it really easy. You're a good friend, Jade."

"Aw, likewise," I replied.

Cori nudged my shoulder just as the dolphins swam over to the thirteen-year-old girl, Macy, and her little brother, Nick.

John the trainer rubbed the top of one of the dolphin's heads and whispered something then smiled at Nick.

The dolphins calmed right down around Nick instead of splashing and calling out for fish. One of them rolled over onto its back so Nick could pat its belly.

"Go ahead, Nick," John said quietly. "You can pet him if you like."

Nick held out his hand to pat the dolphin's belly. For the first time since he joined our group, I thought I saw Nick smile. John offered him the bucket of fish. Nick took one shyly and held it in his hand for the dolphin to take.

Fish!

I shook my head, laughing to myself that of all the superpowers I could have gotten out of this whole mer thing, it had to be the ability to communicate with an animal I'd probably never see again. Why not a cat or a dog? I could make a killing if I could communicate with household pets. I could imagine people paying good money to find out what was going on inside Whiskers's or Fido's head.

Instead I ended up being the completely useless Dolphin Whisperer.

I looked up at the blazing sun overhead, wishing I'd worn a hat because the part between my new braids was starting to get hot. I wondered what time it was, and I was about to ask Cori, but she was busy with one of the dolphins. Then I saw that Macy was wearing a waterproof watch.

"Would you mind telling me what time it is?" I asked.

Macy looked at her watch and smiled brightly. "It's two forty-five."

"Thanks," I said, thinking that Luke and Trey should be landing at the airport at any time. Then I watched Nick pull back his hand again when the trainer told him he could hug the dolphin if he wanted.

"Is your brother okay?" I asked.

"Yeah, he's okay," Macy said. "He's just been in the hospital a lot lately, so this is all kind of new for him."

"So it's your first time here?" I asked. "Me too."

"Everyone's been really nice, and the concert Friday night will be the icing on the cake. Taylor 'n Tyler are Nick's favorite."

"There's a concert Friday night?" Cori interrupted. I could tell that despite the hate she'd had for them since they sang her and Trey's song, she was still very much a fan.

"Yeah, but it's a private concert, I think. Just for the other Sparkle Wishers," Macy replied.

"Sparkle Wishers?" I asked. Then it finally came to me. "Like the Sparkle Wish Club?"

The Sparkle Wish Club granted wishes to critically ill kids. It sounded like the club had flown Nick and his family to the Bahamas to go to Taylor 'n Tyler's benefit concert.

Despite the fact that Taylor 'n Tyler probably took our reservation at the Eutopia without knowing, I was beginning to think they were pretty good guys.

"Yeah," Macy replied. "Coming here to see Taylor 'n Tyler was Nick's Sparkle Wish. That and swimming with the dolphins."

"Those are some pretty great wishes," I said.

"We've had to back out once before because he wasn't well enough to come, but when they got a cancellation last week, they invited us plus our two sets of grandparents," Macy said.

"Are they all here with you?" I asked. "My gran was supposed to come with us but she couldn't travel."

"No, we thought they might come so we got concert tickets for everyone, but it's just us and our parents after all," Macy replied. "We still have the four extra tickets if you want them for you and your friends."

"No, that's okay," Cori said quickly. She was still bitter about Taylor 'n Tyler ruining our Eutopia experience.

"Well, let me know if you change your mind," Macy said.

By then, the dolphins had all been herded and they were giving the campers tow rides on boogie boards. I handed a boogie board to Nick with a smile.

"Time to make this part of your wish come true, buddy."

Once the dolphins had finished their show at the end of the day, Cori and I helped the trainers collect the wet suits and gear from some of the younger participants. We brought the equipment over to a row of hooks on a nearby shed to hang them up to dry.

"It must be really cool to work with dolphins like that," I said as I handed a few face masks to John, our dolphin trainer. "You really have a way with them."

"I guess it was something I was always meant to do," John said with a smile. "Even though I almost messed it up."

"What do you mean?" I asked.

John was thoughtful for a moment as if trying to decide how to phrase something. "Well, I was once in a really dark place and couldn't see my way through. It was only with the help of a good friend and these dolphins that I survived. It's kind of like a wish I never knew I had came true."

"Sort of like that little guy Nick," I said. "You really had a way with him too."

John flushed with embarrassment. "It wasn't me. The dolphins somehow know when they need to take special care. I just give gentle guidance."

I thought about that for a second. Did the dolphins somehow know Nick was sick? If I could somewhat understand them, could the dolphins also understand humans?

Cori must have picked up on that too, because she piped up.

"Hey, John. Do you think dolphins can understand humans? Like understand what we're saying and stuff like that?" she asked.

I nudged her. "What are you doing?"

"Just asking a question," she muttered back.

John laughed, then joined his other trainers, but he called over his shoulder. "Let's just say—dolphins and humans probably aren't as different as we think."

"So there you have it," Cori said as she walked back to the water's edge to get her bag and flip-flops. "Maybe you *can* talk to dolphins after all, lucky girl."

I laughed and listened for any more squeaks or calls from the dolphins, but they were either full of fish or tuckered out from their day of shows. All I could hear were the whistle of the wind and the sound of waves lapping up on shore.

"Hey, guys!" I heard a voice behind us.

I turned to see two very familiar guys walking down the beach toward me.

"Luke! Trey!" I ran up to Luke and gave him a big hug. "You guys made it!"

"Yeah," Luke said, nodding back to the Eutopia. "Our mom and dad are just checking in. The Teen Club people said we'd find you guys here."

I turned to look for Cori by the water's edge, but she was taking her time rinsing out her flip-flops.

"Hey, Cori. Look who it is!"

Cori looked back from the conversation she was having with Macy. They'd connected in a big-sister, little-sister way ever since we found out about Nick and the Sparkle Wish Club.

"Hey, there," Cori said. She took a little while to put on her flip-flops and say good-bye to Macy before heading up the beach to us.

"Um, hi, Cori," Trey said, giving her an awkward hug. I'd never seen him so unsure of himself. Where was the happy-go-lucky Trey we all knew and loved?

"Hey," Cori said.

"So," Luke said enthusiastically. "Your parents texted mine, and we're supposed to meet for dinner at a place called the Crab Shack at six. They asked us to walk you back to your hotel so you could get ready."

"Perfect. I need to send an email before we go anyway," I said.

"The Crab Shack, huh? So, like a date?" Cori asked. She snuck a look at Trey.

"Should I have brought a corsage?" Trey joked, trying to lighten the mood.

"*Argh...*" Cori stalked away, en route to the Asylum.

"Hey, wait up! Cori..." Trey said, following behind. "I was only kidding!"

"Is it going to be awkward like this for the rest of the trip?" I asked Luke as we followed them in the direction of the hotel.

"Looks like things are heading that way," he replied.

Chapter Eleven

Y OU'RE NOT GOING TO get Internet here," Cori
whispered as I held up my phone on the off chance I
could pick up a stray Wi-Fi signal at the Crab Shack. "You
might as well put your phone away."

I'd sent an email about Dillon's boat to Rayelle back at
the hotel, but she hadn't replied yet. Mom caught my eye
and shook her head, giving me the signal to put my phone
away too, so I stuck it in my bag and grabbed a french fry
from my plate.

"I think I'm officially stuffed." Dad wiped his mouth
with a napkin and smiled contentedly as we finished our
meals. "How did I survive this trip without coming here
before now?"

The Crab Shack was a cozy restaurant overlooking the
ocean, a mile or so down the beach from the Asylum and
the Eutopia. Delicious garlic and oil smells wafted from the
open kitchen where sounds of clanging pots and pans and
sizzling food echoed through the restaurant as chefs cooked
the evening's meals. It was about eight in the evening, and
we sat by a wall of windows overlooking the ocean where
the sun hung low over the horizon.

"The food *is* rather delicious," Mom agreed, popping a

last forkful of crab cake in her mouth. "I've really missed my seafood diet, so this week has been a treat."

I wasn't as much of a seafood nut as Mom, but I'd had the deep-fried shrimp and french fries, and I had to admit it was probably the best meal I'd had since we touched down in Nassau. Hard as it was to believe, this was Wednesday night. We were already halfway through our vacation. Now that the Martins were there, Mom and Dad looked even more relaxed.

Cori, me, Mom, and Mrs. Martin lingered at the table to discuss the wedding, while Dad, Trey, Luke, and Mr. Martin took their desserts to the bar area to catch the football game on the big screen.

"And so like I was saying," Mom said as she finished telling Mrs. Martin about the troubles they'd had with reservations, "we got the marriage license and have the gazebo booked, but without anyone to marry us, the wedding won't be much of a wedding, I'm afraid."

"Oh, that's really too bad," Mrs. Martin replied, setting down her dessert fork. She looked so relaxed and healthy compared to earlier that spring when she'd been in the hospital for epilepsy. In fact, this vacation seemed to be having a positive effect on everyone in our group. "But honestly, we're just happy to spend this time with you. It's a relief after the spring and summer we've all just had."

"You're not kidding!" I said, and everybody laughed.

"Yeah," Cori agreed, stealing a french fry from my plate. "We had to fly partway across the globe but I think it was worth it." Then she scanned the bar area where Trey was throwing darts with Luke and muttered to me. "Well, for the most part anyway."

"So how was the catamaran sailing today, Mom?" I piped up before anyone could catch on to what Cori had said.

"Amazing," Mom said. "We fished for part of the morning then sailed to a remote island where they had a grill with a chef to cook our catch." I could tell Mom and Dad had had a great time, and I was relieved they were getting to enjoy their vacation, despite the pain of not being able to find someone to perform their wedding ceremony.

"Oh, that sounds lovely!" Mrs. Martin said. "I've never been on a catamaran."

"Maybe you guys can all go out again tomorrow," I suggested as an evil plan began to form in my mind. I needed a way to get this vacation back on track for Cori and Trey, and I was determined to do it even if it meant locking them in a room together. "Cori and I can just hang back and chill out with Luke and Trey around the pool, right, Cori?" I asked, giving her an encouraging look.

She didn't look convinced.

"I'm not sure I'm ready to let the Martin brothers loose in the Bahamas twenty-four hours after touching down," Mrs. Martin said with a laugh.

"As long as you don't drag them around the local shipyard, they should be fine," Cori said under her breath to me.

"Shh." I nudged Cori's arm.

"Oh, they have this great thing called the Teen Club at the Eutopia," Mom said. "Cori and Jade had a wonderful time there today, didn't you, girls?"

"Yeah, we helped train dolphins today—it was so much fun!" Cori said, coming back to life.

Perfect. I looked at Cori and smiled, coming up with a plan to get her and Trey talking again. It had been kind of tense since we'd all gotten back together earlier. I wasn't quite sure if they were speaking or not, but if Cori and Trey didn't get it together, the next few days of fun in the sun might turn out to be a bit of a bust.

"The Teen Club is really well run," Mom assured Mrs. Martin. "If you're okay with it, they can do that and we can go out on the catamaran together."

"What are we doing, exactly?" Trey asked as he and Luke came back to the table to sit down after their round of darts.

"We were just saying we can do Teen Club again tomorrow while our parents take a catamaran ride," I suggested.

"Sounds good to me," Luke said.

"I'm in," Trey agreed.

"Okay, that actually sounds great," Mrs. Martin said, then turned to Mom. "Micci, if you book the catamaran, I'll take care of the kids' registrations once we get back to the Eutopia."

"Were you guys planning on heading back to the hotels now?" I asked.

"Well, it would be cruel to leave at this stage in the game." Mom glanced over to the bar where Dad and Mr.

Martin were. Someone scored and they both cheered. "I think we'll wait until the fourth quarter's finished if you don't mind."

"Is it okay if we all walk back and meet you guys at the hotel?" Luke asked his mom.

"Yeah, we'll be at the arcade," Trey said rubbing his hands together. "I still need to beat my high score at King Kong Krush."

Cori rolled her eyes.

"As long as you stick together," Mom said.

"Yeah, okay with me too. We'll see you there in an hour or so," Mrs. Martin said.

Luke and I hung back a few dozen feet behind Cori and Trey as we walked along the beach on the way back to our hotels. The sun hung low in the sky and reflected pink and orange ripples along the water. The wind had picked up, and it blew my hair across my face.

Luke looked over and pushed my hair back behind my ear as we waded ankle deep through the water. "Did I tell you I like your braids?"

"Thanks," I replied. "Trying to soak in the local culture and all. Our new friend Rayelle's cousin did them for us."

"I hope this wind is good for sailing," Luke said. "We talked to my grandpa yesterday, and he and Bobbie should be getting here on Friday night."

If we could get Cori's parents here and Bobbie and Eddie, our wedding party would be complete.

"Oh, good. Mom wasn't sure if they'd make it on time," I said. "Speaking of Bobbie—what was the water like in Florida when you were there last spring?"

"It was warmer than the water around Port Toulouse, if that's what you're asking," Luke said.

"I figured that," I said, whacking him in the arm. "I mean are there tropical fish and coral like around here? Oh, and did you see any dolphins?"

"We were on the Atlantic coast so there were plenty of cool fish, but I didn't see any dolphins. I've actually never seen one," Luke said.

"What's up with that, anyway? I hadn't seen a dolphin before today either. You'd think one of us would have come across one, given our secret identities," I said.

"Bobbie once told me that mers and dolphins don't usually live in the same habitat," Luke said. "Apparently, mer rings are like kryptonite to dolphins so they just evolved to stay away."

"The dolphins at Dolphin Lagoon were weird with me at first, but then I think one of them called me 'dude,'" I said.

"*Dude?*" Luke said with a laugh as we continued to splash through the water along the edge of the beach.

"That's what it sounded like, anyway." All of a sudden, out of the corner of my eye, I saw a fin emerge from the water a few hundred feet offshore. "Oh!" I said, stopping in place and pointing for Luke to see. "Did you see that?"

Luke shaded his eyes against the setting sun and looked out over the horizon.

"Is that a dolphin or a shark?" he asked.

"I hope it's not a shark!" I froze for a moment. Should we get out of the ocean? Could sharks swim in ankle-deep water? It took a second but instead of a shark, to my relief, a long, slim, silver beak surfaced, followed by a fin. "Cori showed me this video from one of the shark dives they do around here. It was gruesome!"

"Oh, dolphins! Hey, cool—I think there are two of them," Luke said as another fin surfaced.

"I wonder if I can hear them again." I strained my ears to listen, but all I could hear were the whistling wind and the sound of the waves lapping around our ankles.

"Hear the dolphins?" Luke asked. "Do they make much of a sound?"

We listened together a bit longer, and I thought I could make out a few squeaks and squeals but nothing that sounded like a word.

"What did you say?" Luke turned to me.

"Huh?" I asked. "I didn't say anything."

I listened to see if I could hear what Luke heard.

Free…swim…free…

"That's them!" I exclaimed, hearing the dolphins' voices.

"Who?" Luke asked.

"The dolphins," I said with a wide smile. "Like when one of them called me 'dude' earlier. I can understand them."

"That's amazing!" Luke said, and he listened some more.

Help…swim…free…

"Hey, that's cool. I think I can understand them too."

Luke shaded his eyes again to watch the dolphins but they soon swam off into the distance.

"I wonder what they're trying to say," I said.

"Not sure. Maybe they're being *chased* by the sharks?" Luke took my hand again and we continued down along the beach. Trey and Cori had gotten a little ahead of us so we picked up the pace.

"Well, at least we know there aren't any mers around the Bahamas if it's chock-full of dolphins," I added.

"It's kind of cool being in a mer-free zone for a change," Luke said, squeezing my hand. "Present company excluded."

"Of course," I agreed.

It was nice to know that Luke and my Video Gab conversation back in the elevator was a thing of the past. Now we could just talk and hang out in a no-stress, no-drama way.

I actually thought we were about to have that moonlit kiss we'd talked about, but the moment was ruined by a ruckus from farther down the beach. Cori and Trey had stopped and were facing each other.

"You just don't get it!" Cori yelled.

"Get what?" Trey said. "Because if there's some kind of boyfriend rule book I don't know about, please clue me in."

"Clue you in? That's the whole problem!" Cori replied.

There was a lot of arm waving and shouting; then Cori turned and stalked away and Trey was left standing at the edge of the water, shaking his head.

"I thought they were getting along." Luke nodded toward Cori and Trey.

"Right," I said offhandedly, "until your brother makes another boneheaded move."

It was out of my mouth before I could stop it. I couldn't help it—Cori was my girl. She'd had my back so many times in the past year that I owed her my life, more than once, so when it came to Cori, I was like a mama bear and her cub.

Luke looked at me with a crushed look on his face.

"Sorry, I should go check on Trey." He dropped my hand and ran ahead. "Hey, bro! Wait up."

So much for that moonlit kiss.

Chapter Twelve

I GOT OUT OF BED on Thursday morning hoping this was the day everything would finally come together. Good news on the wedding front, less weirdness on the Luke front, and some kind of cease-fire on the Cori and Trey front would have been pretty darn awesome just about then.

The night before had been a dud. Cori, Trey, Luke, and I had hung out at the arcade, speaking in one-word sentences until our parents got there, and everyone went to bed early. Talk about partying it up in the Bahamas!

The only silver lining was that Cori spotted Taylor 'n Tyler getting into a limo when we were on our way back to the Asylum, and she convinced me to get an autograph for Macy's little brother, Nick, as a souvenir of his Sparkle Wish trip while she hid behind a plant at the front entry so the bodyguards wouldn't recognize her as the crazy, cell-phone-waving beach stalker.

I listened to see if Mom and Dad were up in the room next door. I could hear them talking, so I hopped in our shower before Cori woke up, beating her to the punch for once on this trip.

"Yeowch!" Only problem was that the scalp between

my braids was tender and sunburned, and the spray of the shower stung so badly that I had to keep jumping in and out of the water. I was half tempted to take out the braids just to give my scalp a break, but I knew Cori would kill me because she'd wanted to get braids together ever since she found out we were coming to the Bahamas.

Plus, Kiki's braids really were works of art and I wanted to make sure I still had them when we got back to Port Toulouse so everyone, including the rude ladies at Dooley's Drugstore, would remember where we'd gone and why we'd been there. Just the thought of their smug faces made me hope everything worked out for the wedding so we could come back to Port Toulouse and rub the "scandal" in their faces.

I was standing in front of the bathroom mirror smearing aloe vera gel on my scalp after my shower when my phone buzzed on the counter with an email alert. Yes, I'd gotten stuck in the Elevator of Doom and it was like a twenty-four-hour frat party at the Asylum, but thank goodness for hotel Wi-Fi. Odds were, Luke had Internet at the Eutopia too. Was he emailing to smooth things over after he'd pretty much abandoned me on the beach the night before?

I picked up my phone, hoping it was him, but it was Rayelle.

"Oh." She was probably emailing about Dillon.

Hi Jade,

Sorry for taking so long but I wanted to check out a few things before I got back to you. Apparently, Dillon hasn't been around for three days but his mom thinks he's crashing at Kiki's boyfriend's house— not that she usually cares where he is as long as he brings home money, but that's another story. If he's not there and actually doing something stupid, I'm afraid he's going to get into a lot of trouble. He doesn't have the best track record but I owe him so I really need help. Problem is, I have school and I can't get hold of Kiki. Could you please see if you can find Kiki on the beach and ask if her boyfriend has seen Dillon?

—Rayelle

I did the mental math. Three days meant Dillon had been missing since we had that run-in about the Wonderment cruise ship on Monday. He hadn't been at the Straw Market on Tuesday when I went looking for him either, but Rayelle had seen Officer Ensel talking with the guy from the cruise ship, hadn't she? The police were obviously on the case. So what was Dillon's deal?

One way or another, Rayelle had been super nice to me and Cori. The least I could do was go check things out with Kiki. I looked at the time on my phone, and it was 8:02 a.m. If we hurried, we could scoot down the beach, talk to Kiki, and make it back for breakfast before Teen Club.

Hi Rayelle,

I'll see what I can find out and get back to you as soon as I can. My email only works in the hotel, though, so it might take me a while to reply. Try not to worry. I'm sure Dillon is okay.

—Jade

I finished getting dressed and went back into the room. Cori was sitting up in her bed staring at her phone.

"Up and at 'em," I said, combing my wet hair before it turned into a bird's nest.

Cori hadn't moved and was still staring at her phone.

"What's going on?" I asked.

"My phone is dead," Cori said. Without the charger, there was no way of recharging her phone.

"Too many shark videos, huh?" I joked.

"What if Trey tried to email or Video Gab with me?" she asked.

"Do you want him to?" I asked. "I mean, things got a little tense last night on the beach."

"Argh!" Cori sighed in frustration. "If he could just act like a normal boyfriend instead of being so goofy all the time. Last night on the beach I told him the moon reminded me of how we roasted marshmallows at your gran's cottage this summer then hung out under the stars at the end of the pier, and *he* told me how he once stuffed twelve marshmallows in his mouth.'"

I laughed out loud, visualizing Trey with his cheeks all puffed up like a chipmunk getting ready for winter.

"Yeah, but that's Trey, though, right?" I asked.

"That's the problem! He's so…so…Trey-ish!" Cori said. "Anyway, how am I supposed to survive without my phone?" she asked, looking up at me like a puppy who'd lost its mommy.

"I'm sure you'll live. Get dressed!" I said. "We're going on a quest."

"Not the shipyard again!" Cori protested.

"No, nothing like that. Look, I'll even tell my parents where we're going if it makes you feel better." I knocked on the adjoining door to Mom and Dad's room. Their catamaran ride didn't start until a little later, so they didn't have to rush out the door at the crack of dawn like the day before. "Hey, guys?" I called out.

"Good morning!" Mom opened the door and popped her head into our room.

"Is it okay if Cori and I go for a walk on the beach before breakfast?" I asked. "Rayelle wants us to get a message to her cousin Kiki. The girl who did our braids."

"Just stay together and don't go in the water," Mom said with a wink.

Go in the water? Yeah. No fear of that.

Cori and I saw a few couples walking along the beach during our half-mile walk from the Asylum to the Eutopia, but the gray skies and a cool morning wind were keeping most people inside.

By the time we reached the cabana where Kiki worked, I could see her huddled inside, wrapped up in a blanket with no customers in sight.

"Slow morning?" I asked as we walked up to her booth.

"Ah, Rayelle's friends." Kiki greeted us with a beaming smile. "Come back for more braids?"

"Not exactly," I said sheepishly. "Rayelle's been trying to get hold of you."

"That girl," Kiki said, shaking her head. "I've been ignoring her. I keep telling her to forget about that guy Dillon."

"So you've been getting her texts?" I asked. But apparently not answering them.

"It won't do her no good to keep messing with him," Kiki said, waving her hand through the air.

"She just wants to know if your boyfriend has seen Dillon or not. He's been missing since Monday," I replied.

"Missing or messing around?" Kiki shook her head. "Listen. I know Dillon ain't got it very good with his dad out of the picture and his mom trying to make ends meet and all. Heck, Dillon is the best conch diver on the island, and he's keeping that family afloat. He's just been losing his way lately. Rayelle is a good girl. I just don't want to see her get mixed up with someone like him."

Cori nudged my arm and whispered in my ear, "Come on. This isn't getting us anywhere."

"No wait, Cori," I whispered back. I turned to Kiki. "So you're saying your boyfriend hasn't seen him?"

"Ask him yourself. He should be at Dolphin Lagoon getting ready for the first show. His name is John."

"John, as in the dolphin trainer John?" Cori asked as we cut through the glittering lobby of the Eutopia to get to the other end of the resort where Dolphin Lagoon was.

"I guess," I replied.

We spotted John by the equipment shed, handing out wet suits and life jackets to the guests.

"Do you think we should bother him?" I asked, checking my phone. It was already eight-thirty, and we were cutting it close if we wanted breakfast before Teen Club. I internally scolded myself for thinking about food at a time like this. Rayelle had asked me for help and I planned on doing everything I could to put her mind at ease. I had to admit that I was kind of worried about Dillon too, even though I didn't know him very well.

"John?" I asked as we approached.

John turned our way and smiled. "Ah Jade, right? And Cori?"

"Good memory," Cori said.

"Can we ask you something?" I asked.

"Sure, but I only have a few seconds," he said, nodding to the waiting dolphins in the lagoon.

"Our friend Rayelle wanted to know if you've seen Dillon. His mom thinks he's staying with you," I said.

"Dillon?" John scratched his chin. "I haven't seen him since Monday night."

I knew didn't have much time so I had to work fast.

"What did he say to you when he asked you to sneak onto the cruise ship?" I asked.

John looked around to make sure no one was listening.

"Look, I'm not sure what Dillon was up to, but whatever it was, it wasn't to steal anything if that's what you're thinking," John said as the other trainer waved him over to start the show. "Sorry, I gotta go."

"Thanks," I said as he walked away.

The dolphin trainers all grouped together for a pre-show powwow, and one of the dolphins swam up to where they were standing and splashed John.

Hello!

My eyes popped open in surprise. It was the dolphin talking again. Meanwhile, John had turned to smile and wave the dolphin away.

Could John understand what the dolphin was saying? I wondered. No…that was just a coincidence.

"So, where the heck is Dillon, then?" Cori asked as we headed back to the Asylum, hoping they hadn't packed up breakfast yet.

"I'm not sure," I said. But something on the horizon of

the lagoon caught my eye. It was a large, white ship with a big W on the top. The Wonderment Cruiselines ship.

It was back.

We grabbed a couple bananas and yogurt cups from the Asylum's buffet table and headed back up the elevator to our room. I threw my stuff on the bed and grabbed my phone to search for Rayelle's email so I could reply.

Hi Rayelle,

We talked to Kiki's boyfriend, John, and he hasn't seen Dillon since Monday night. I don't know what that means exactly, but I'm sorry I don't have better news. What do you think we should do now?

—Jade

Cori was reading over my shoulder and sighed.

"What?" I asked.

"You did what she asked. Now just let it go. Your parents are supposed to get married Saturday. Don't you think you have better things to do with your time than getting dragged into the local teen drama?" Cori asked.

"Yeah, like our own teen drama isn't enough to deal with, right?" I muttered. I thought back to what Cori had said earlier about Trey being too Trey-ish.

"What's that supposed to mean?" Cori asked.

Should I say something? Or was Luke right when he said we should just stay out of it?

"Nothing. Forget it," I said.

My email alert sound went off.

Hi Jade,

Can't write now because I'm in school and will get killed if they catch me texting. I just don't know what to do.

—Rayelle

My heart went out to her, but I really didn't know what to do either.

Let me talk to my mom and dad. Maybe they'll have an idea.

—Jade

I knocked on Mom and Dad's door and explained everything to them while they finished getting ready for their catamaran excursion.

"I think we should call that Officer Ensel guy," Dad said.

"But Rayelle doesn't want to get Dillon in trouble," I said. Maybe it hadn't been such a good idea to tell my parents.

"Yes, but if he's already in trouble, isn't it better if someone he knows helps him?" Mom asked.

"I guess," I said, going through my bag for Officer Ensel's card. I gave Dad Faye's card by mistake then found the right one and handed it to him. He dialed the number and gave the card back to me.

"Rayelle's not going to like this," I whispered to Cori while Dad was on the phone.

"It's better to let someone else deal with it," Cori said. "What do we really know about this guy anyway?"

"I hope you're right," I said.

Dad chatted on the phone for a few minutes, then hung up and grabbed his floppy, straw sun hat. "Okay, everyone. That's done. Officer Ensel is going to look into it and has assured me they will do everything they can—and he said he'd try to be discreet about it."

So that was that. Officer Ensel would find out what happened to Dillon, if anything, and he'd try to keep it on the down-low. Rayelle would be relieved to hear that, and I could finally put it out of my head with good conscience.

"We should head out. Our shuttle to the catamaran leaves in five minutes," Mom said.

"And we can drop you off at the Eutopia to meet Luke and Trey when we pick up the Martins," Dad replied. He clapped his hands for us to hustle. "Let's go, let's go. We've got some fish to fry!"

"All right, hold on. We're coming!" I grabbed my stuff from my bed and followed them out the door.

It wasn't until I was in the shuttle on my way to the Eutopia that I remembered I'd left my phone on the nightstand in the hotel room at the Asylum.

And I'd forgotten to email Rayelle to let her know that Officer Ensel was on the case.

Chapter Thirteen

I HUNTED THROUGH MY BAG once we got to Teen Club, checking one last time for my cell phone, but all I came up with were a couple of business cards and scraps of paper.

"Okay, everyone!" Marissa, the Teen Club coordinator, said as she scanned her clipboard. "Fourteen-year-olds and up for Group A today. Ten- to thirteen-year-olds in Group B, and Chance will be in charge of the nine and unders."

"Aw, too bad," Cori said. "I was kind of looking forward to seeing Nick and Macy."

"Yeah. Oh, and I still have that Taylor 'n Tyler autograph for Nick," I said, holding up the paper.

I kept searching through my bag, willing my phone to appear. "I can't believe I forgot to email Rayelle back. Now I won't be able to get in touch with her until we get back to the hotel later."

"Just ask Luke for his phone when he gets here," Cori said.

"That's the problem, though," I said. "I don't remember her email address."

"Seriously, Jade?" Cori said. "You've got to let this go. Remember what I told you on the airplane?"

"Yeah?" I said skeptically.

"Not everything is a life-or-death emergency. We're on vacation to relax and have fun. Remember?" Cori asked.

"I remember. But do you remember?" I asked. "The 'have fun' part, I mean."

Cori looked at me and scowled. "I know you're talking about Trey, but honestly, the guy just doesn't get it."

I thought back to the last thing I'd said about Trey to Luke on the beach, about him being boneheaded. It kind of felt like we were ganging up on Trey—well, at least Cori and I were—for just being...Trey. But how could I say that to Cori?

"Listen, Cori," I said quietly. "Maybe you're expecting too much from Trey."

"Is it too much to ask to have a boyfriend act like a boyfriend?" Cori asked.

"No, that's not what I meant," I said, trying to figure out what I actually did mean. "It's just—"

"Forget it," Cori said. "You have Luke, and everything is all hunky-dory for you guys. I guess I'm just not that lucky."

"Cori, it's not..." I said, regretting I'd said anything at all.

But by then, Luke and Trey had arrived, and the Teen Club was on the move to our next thrilling adventure.

The weirdest thing happened when we arrived at Dolphin Lagoon. Anytime Luke got close to the dolphins, they freaked out and swam in the other direction.

The dolphins were acting so strange and upset that the rest of the dolphin activity had to be canceled and we were stuck at the waterslides for the rest of the afternoon.

Our parents picked us up from Teen Club later that day, and we went straight to dinner at the Eutopia with the Martins. Then we headed to the marina to meet Bobbie and Eddie at their sailboat for dessert. The marina was near the bridge that spanned the harbor between Nassau and Paradise Island, not far from where the cruise ships were docked at the shipyard.

"The Eutopia sure knows how to lay out a delicious spread. What a meal," Dad exclaimed as he patted his belly while we walked along the series of docks to Bobbie's sailboat.

"Better than the cafeteria line at the Asylum," I agreed under my breath.

It was nightfall by then and the marina was lit up with strings of white lights like a Christmas tree, adding to the cheery feeling of the evening.

"Those dolphins at Dolphin Lagoon did *not* like you," I said to Luke as we hung back with Trey and Cori behind the adults in the group. Bobbie wasn't kidding when she told Luke dolphins and mers didn't mix.

"How do you know it was me?" Luke asked. "You're a mer too."

"They were totally fine with me yesterday," I teased, thinking I wasn't *as* annoying to dolphins because I was part human. "Well, they acted a little weird at first, but I think I have the whole 'part-human' thing going for me. In fact, I'm kind of a Dolphin Whisperer. You're the one who had them all huddled on the far side of the lagoon today."

"What can I say?" Luke said with a smirk. "Just call me the Dolphin Hollerer."

"You could get that on a T-shirt," I suggested.

Luke held my hand, away from Dad's prying, overprotective eye, and I wondered if he had put our conversation on the beach from the night before behind him. Honestly, that was fine with me. In fact, I tried to block out all the weirdness the trip had brought so far with Dillon and Rayelle, and the tension between Cori and Trey, and relaxed into the moment.

"It's so pretty," Cori said as we walked along the main dock of the marina, looking for the branch of the jetty where Bobbie's sailboat was berthed. "Almost romantic."

"Oh, look at that boat!" Trey ran ahead and pointed to a hundred-foot yacht. "Four decks, a flying bridge, and a hot tub. That is so *sick*…"

"See what I mean?" Cori muttered to me.

We turned down one of the branches of the jetty, and soon we reached a dark blue wooden sailboat.

"This is it. Ahoy!" Dad called out as we arrived at the boat.

"Did Bobbie and Eddie really sail all the way from Florida on this thing?" I asked. The boat was about thirty feet long with gleaming hardwood decking. Its white sails were wrapped around two tall wooden masts. I envisioned the boat being pitched around the ocean like a wine cork in a bucket of water. If a three-hour flight had my stomach in spasms, I could only imagine what sailing across the open ocean in a wooden schooner would do for my intestinal tract.

"Hard to imagine, huh?" Luke asked. "But we sailed all the way from Port Toulouse to Florida last spring, remember? And our boat is only a few feet longer than this one."

I thought back to when I'd first seen Luke at Dooley's Drugstore when he returned from his sailing trip that spring. Everyone at school thought his family had gone on an adventurous sailing expedition—which was partly true—but mostly they had gone to Florida because Eddie's friend Bobbie was a Webbed One (which is a human that started off as a mer). She'd helped Luke with his first human-to-mer transition.

"Ahoy!" Eddie replied, popping his head out from the lower deck and waving us aboard.

A pretty, middle-aged woman with graying hair emerged from the cabin behind Eddie. Bobbie and Eddie were probably the biggest mer experts in the world. They'd been working together for many years, ever since Eddie was laughed off a Florida university's faculty for publishing an article about mers in a scientific journal. Now he preferred to keep his mer knowledge a secret and urged us all to do the same.

"Bobbie!" Luke said, hopping aboard to give his mentor a big hug.

"Luke! I swear you've grown a foot since last spring," Bobbie said, holding him at arm's length to get a good look at him.

Luke blushed. "Well, not quite a foot but an inch or two, I suppose."

Eddie introduced Bobbie to me, Cori, and Mom and Dad, and we all sat around the upper deck under the twilight of the moon and chatted.

"So what have you all been doing with yourselves on this lovely island?" Bobbie asked as she served the delicious coconut dessert she'd picked up from a local island bakery.

"Dolphins, dolphins, and more dolphins," Cori said, beaming as she took the plate Bobbie offered.

"Aren't they the most magnificent creatures?" Bobbie asked.

"Speaking of which," I interrupted, "Luke was telling me about the link between dolphins and mers. That they can't coexist in the same habitat?"

Bobbie looked impressed and turned to Luke.

"I didn't realize you were listening when I was boring you with all that mer trivia," she replied. "We haven't been able to pinpoint the exact cause, but our best guess is that it has something to do with the natural frequency mers produce."

"You mean the thing that keeps passing boats from seeing mers on their sonar?" I asked.

"Yes. Dolphins can't seem to process the sound and find it painful," Eddie chimed in.

"So, I'm just wondering," I continued, "have there ever been any mers reported in the Bahamas?"

"Jade…" Cori muttered.

"What?" I asked. "I'm just curious."

Bobbie shook her head. "Florida is the southernmost boundary for mer activity, as far as we know."

"But aren't there dolphins in Florida too?" I asked.

"Yes but not in the pockets of ocean where mers have staked their claim. Mers tend to stick to very limited territories so it's usually not much of a problem."

"They just kind of ignore each other," Eddie added. Then he winked. "It's a big ocean."

"Is it possible, though, that mers and dolphins share a similar language?" I asked.

"Jade?" Mom asked. "Where is this all coming from?"

Uh-oh. Maybe I should dial it back a bit. I had promised Mom and Cori to give this mer stuff a rest this week, but the weird encounter at Dolphin Lagoon had me thinking. Maybe I should just play it cool.

Who was I kidding? I didn't know *how* to play it cool.

"It's just that I thought I could understand what the dolphins were saying back at Dolphin Lagoon," I replied.

"Well, that's interesting," Bobbie said. "I haven't really studied the phenomenon, but I suppose it's possible for mers and dolphins to share some language similarities."

"Okay, cool," I said, dropping the subject.

The conversation turned to everyone wanting to know about the sailing trip from Florida. Bobbie and Eddie kept everyone entertained with their tales of canned soup lunches, circling sharks, and the time they intercepted a CB radio message from drug smugglers.

"So we called it in to the Coast Guard and they picked them up near Miami," Bobbie said.

"The smugglers are getting craftier and craftier with their schemes so it was nice to help catch one in the act," Eddie added.

"Sweet. Up high!" Trey said, giving his grandfather a high five.

"He thinks everything deserves a high five," Cori muttered to me, and I could tell it was time to go stretch our legs.

The boat really wasn't meant for a crowd, so when Bobbie went into the cabin to retrieve a bottle of wine and glasses and the conversation turned to drug legislation and gun control, I took it as a cue to make our escape.

"Hey," I said, turning to Mom, "is it okay if Cori, I, and the guys take a walk around the marina and see if we can spot any celebrities on one of these mega-yachts?"

"It's kind of dark out," Mom said, looking past me to the adjoining docks.

"They have lights everywhere," I said. "We'll stick together. We'll be fine."

"Make sure to take a picture if you see anybody famous." Dad gave me a thumbs-up and settled in with a glass of wine next to Mom.

"Well, we're only staying for another hour so don't go far," Mom said with a smile.

The marina itself was kind of big and confusing with a main dock splitting into smaller docks that berthed several hundred boats.

"I wonder who owns this one," Trey said as he peered through the cheerily lit windows of a gargantuan pleasure craft.

"Oh, maybe Jay Jo is on vacation here to get over her broken heart from Justin," Cori said. She'd obviously studied the celebrity gossip magazines cover to cover since we'd arrived.

We strolled along the main dock and tried to guess who might be in the huge yachts. All of a sudden, a long horn sounded and we looked down the harbor to see what it was.

A humongous cruise ship was in the process of docking next to a very familiar-looking boat farther down at the shipyard.

"Hey, isn't that the Wonderment cruise ship?" Cori said.

It was dark, but the large ship's upper decks were lit up enough that we could identify it. Sure enough, the docked ship had a big W emblem and a massive waterslide that spanned out over the upper deck, making my stomach quake.

"I think I saw it leave port yesterday," I said, remembering that we'd spotted the ship from Dolphin Lagoon the day before. "I thought it had left for good. I wonder why it's back."

"When we went on our Alaskan cruise, we made two stops in Anchorage. Maybe it's something like that," Cori said.

"Maybe," I agreed.

"That waterslide looks sick!" Trey exclaimed.

"Now *that's* something we agree on," Cori said. Without thinking, she raised her hand to give Trey a high five then glanced at me with a sheepish look on her face.

"Why are you guys so interested in that Wonderment ship anyway?" Luke asked. "Are you planning a cruise?"

I wasn't sure what to say. "No, nothing like that. It's just this thing that happened when we first got here," I replied. "There's this guy named Dillon who sells conches at the Straw Market. He and I both saw something getting dumped out of a porthole on the cruise ship, and Dillon was convinced it was a dead body."

"Seriously?" Trey said. "That's whacked."

"I'm not saying it was actually a body," I replied, but saying it out loud like that stirred up a new mixture of doubt. "A police officer was there, and he's been investigating."

"And I've been telling her to just forget about it—there's no way you got away from all that mer business in Port Toulouse only to fly halfway around the earth to jump into another pool of craziness," Cori said.

"I know you're right, which is why you'll notice I haven't mentioned it to the guys until now," I said with a satisfied grin.

"That and the penalty of death your father threatened if you did anything to stress your mom out on this trip," Cori joked.

"True," I replied. We walked a bit more and kept up our movie-star watch.

Cori and Trey walked ahead, leaving Luke and me to trail behind walking in silence. Luke squeezed my hand.

"Everything okay?" he asked.

"Yeah," I replied.

"'Cause you seem a little weirded out," Luke said. "And for what it's worth, any time you're weirded out, it's usually for a good reason."

"It's just that this guy Dillon was so convinced he'd seen something."

As I said the words, I spotted a dark shadow on one of the boats leading down a side jetty. The person looked my way. His face was in shadows and it took me a half second to register what kind of hat he was wearing. But before I could call out, he dove overboard, hat and all, and disappeared into the dark, inky water without making so much as a splash.

"Holy moley! Did you guys see that?" I yelled and pointed at the boat.

Trey and Cori turned to see what I was talking about.

"What?" Luke asked, trying to see what I'd just seen.

"Someone just jumped overboard from that boat over there!" I called out as I ran toward the boat. I was grabbing the ladder to climb down onto the boat's deck when Luke caught up to me and grasped my arm.

"Jade! You can't just go down there. Someone owns that boat. That's trespassing," Luke said. "If you think you saw something, let's just call for help."

"None of our phones work in the Bahamas, remember?"

I touched down on the deck and crossed to the other side of the boat to see where the guy had dived in. "Besides, we have to do something now before it's too late."

"Jade, wait!" Cori said as she and Trey arrived at the side of the boat with Luke. "Don't do anything stupid. Or wet!"

"Cori, I think we might know this guy."

"Who? Dillon?" Cori asked. She ventured down the ladder too and peered over the side of the boat with me. I spotted a hat in the water and snatched it before it floated away.

"Not Dillon. The guy Rayelle saw talking to Officer Ensel the other day. You know—the one with the Wonderment Cruiselines baseball cap?" I held up the hat, which sported the same white W as the ship.

"Lots of people could own one of these hats," Cori said, taking it in her hand.

"And unless he hit his head or something, he's gotta come up for air sometime," Luke added.

Something jumped out of the water about forty feet away from the docks, scaring me out of my skin.

"It's just a dolphin," Luke called out from the pier where he stood with Trey.

Swim...away...

"It's saying something." I turned and said to Luke, "Do you hear that?"

"Oh, wow! Yeah, but are you sure you actually saw something jump out of the boat and into the water?" Luke asked.

I scanned the water again. What *had* I seen? There were lights on most of the boats, but this one was dark. The only light around was the lamp on the pier that cast dark shadows along the boat's deck.

"I'm not sure." Just like the time Dillon had said he'd seen a body getting dumped from the cruise ship, shivers of doubt rippled through my gut. "Maybe it was just some guy messing around where he doesn't belong who doesn't want to get caught."

"Hey, Jade," Cori called out from the stern. She pointed to a rope tied at the end of the boat. "Look at this."

I followed the rope to a beat-up green speedboat.

"That's Dillon's boat," I replied right before I dove into the water.

Chapter Fourteen

"H AVE YOU GONE COMPLETELY banoonoos? What are you doing?" Cori yelled as I surfaced seconds later.

By then, Luke and Trey had jumped down onto the boat deck and joined in.

"You don't know what's down there," Luke said. "Didn't you say there were sharks around here?"

"Oh, rrrightt…" I said slowly, peering along the surface of the water, hoping a tiger reef whatcha-ma-call-it didn't come jumping out at me, teeth a-blazing. "But they wouldn't come all the way into the harbor, would they, Cori?"

"How should I know?" Cori asked.

"You're supposed to be the shark expert!" I yelled.

"You can always get out of the water," Cori said, crossing her arms.

"No," I decided. "I need to find out what the deal is with this guy."

"Why am I not surprised?" Cori asked.

"But first—turn around!" I ordered Luke and Trey. They kind of figured out what I was up to because, thankfully, they did what I asked.

Also thankfully, I'd flicked off my flip-flops before I dove in, but now I had the job of struggling out of my jean shorts as I treaded water next to the boat. Not an easy task! I left my baggy T-shirt on (of course!) but tossed my shorts to Cori, so they would escape the carnage when I dove back into the watery depths of the harbor and my legs exploded into a tail.

"You've got to be kidding me with this," Cori said as she bundled up my shorts in her hands.

"Yeah, we should really get our parents," Trey called over his shoulder.

"No, wait!" I said as I prepared to dive back underwater to check things out. "They're all the way on the other end of the marina. Just let me see what the heck is going on before we drag everyone over here."

"You're just saying that because you know your mom and dad will freak and insist that you get out of the water," Cori said, putting a hand on her hip. "I know how you operate."

"At least let me go with you," Luke said, and I could tell he was getting ready to take off his shoes.

"Think about that one," I said with a laugh. Because I was only *part* mermaid, all I had to do was climb out of the water and start breathing air to turn back into a human. Luke, on the other hand, was born a mer, so things were much more complicated for him. The only way he could turn back from mer to human was with a special tidal pool that brought tides in and out at the right rate for the transformation to occur. My engineer dad had built a man-made version in our garage with a second hand hot tub, wires, tubes, and a computer, but it wasn't something you could pack for a trip to the Bahamas.

"Yeah, I guess you're right," Luke said.

"Don't worry—I'll be back before you can miss me," I said. Then I dove in again before anyone else could object. The water wrapped around me like a warm blanket, so different from the chilly waters off the coast of Port Toulouse. But just like my mer adventures back home, I knew all I had to do was breathe in a few deep breaths of water and it would be Tail City.

Breathe, I reminded myself. Ocean water stung my throat as it rushed deep into my lungs with each breath. At first I felt like gagging, and I sputtered, trying to cough the water back out, but then my body began to crave my next breath of water as if it were air. I took a few more deep breaths, and soon the ocean rushed around me with the force of my exploding tail.

Arglllup! I rang in my daintiest mermaid voice. There I was once again—Jade the Legless Wonder.

Swim, swim.

The first thing I heard was the ring of the dolphins off in the distance. From what Bobbie had said, dolphins and mers didn't mix so I let them make their getaway, hoping I hadn't bothered them. Hopefully, sharks hated to be around dolphins as much as dolphins hated being around mers.

My eyes stung and I blinked away the harbor water until my sight adjusted to the evening light. I spun around in the warm Caribbean water with the taste of salt in my mouth and moved my tail awkwardly, trying to get the feeling back into it just like when your legs go to sleep after sitting cross-legged for too long.

Luke, can you hear me? I rang up to the boat.

Yeah, he rang back. Trey and Cori probably just heard an annoying low ring, but I knew they'd been around Luke and me long enough to know we were talking to each other in our mer voices. *Are you okay?*

Yeah, I'm fine, I replied. *Tell the others not to worry, okay? I'm getting to be an expert at this*, I joked.

That's what I'm afraid of, he replied, but I could tell he had a smirk on his lips.

I swam under the hull of the boat and along the floating pier, trying to catch a glimpse of the man who'd just dived into the water. He couldn't have gone too far. No human could stay underwater that long.

Unless he was a mer—and if he was a mer, why would he want to jump into the water and get stuck sporting a tail? Were there tidal pools in the Bahamas where mers could be transformed back into humans?

Focus, I told myself. Cori was right. There weren't mers looming on every corner of the Bahamas trying to do me in. I really needed to chill.

I started hunting around the boats and swimming along the maze of piers but after ten minutes or so, I'd seen nothing and had lost vocal contact with Luke. Maybe Cori and the guys were right. With the darkness, the unfamiliar waters, and the risk of decapitation by a large, carnivorous, aquatic animal, this was probably a stupid idea.

Swim, swim.

But maybe…

I swam out of the shelter of the marina's docks toward the source of the dolphins' rings and hunted around the darkened waters to see if I could spot them. A current of water bounced off me like a wave against the shore, alerting me that something was nearby. The dolphins were swimming away from me—I could sense it.

Hey, wait! I rang out. It was the strangest thing, but I could almost feel them slowing down in the distance at the sound of my rings. *Can you hold up? I just want to ask you something.*

There was silence for a few minutes but I could sense the dolphins were still there. I swam a few more dozen feet away from the marina, trying to find them.

Stop, one of the dolphins replied.

The dolphin rings weren't exactly like mer rings. They were more abrupt and squeakier, but I could figure out a bit of what they were saying, like how I could understand simple phrases in French even though I'd only studied Spanish. I could sense the dolphins swimming in circles, planning what to do next.

I just want to talk, I rang out as softly as possible. I didn't want to spook them since they were probably a little freaked to sense a mermaid in their midst.

Danger, another dolphin said, and I could feel it turn away like a nervous horse or a shy puppy.

Whoa, I rang. *Easy does it. I'm not going to hurt you.* I said the next few words slowly so the dolphins could hopefully understand. *Do you know what I am?*

More ripples tickled the scales of my tail. I could tell the dolphins were still on the move, but they were staying close by. I thought I heard more rings from them, but these were harder to understand, as if they were speaking very quickly in nervous chatter. Finally, one of them replied.

Ocean human.

Ocean human? Huh. Okay, close enough, I guess.

Yes, ocean human, I rang. *But have you seen an* actual *human swimming near here? I think he may be in danger.*

Danger, danger. The call came back. I could tell the dolphins were getting agitated by the vibrating energy all around me. It was weird but it felt as though I'd dialed into their frequency—and that frequency was on the high end of "stressed out."

Please, if you could help me, I rang out into the dark waters. *Then I'll leave you alone. I promise.*

A few moments later, a long silver beak appeared in the darkened waters a dozen feet or so away.

Never before, ocean humans, the dolphin rang.

It was obvious the dolphin thought I was a bit of a freak show by the way it swam all around me, inspecting me from all angles. There was also a pained expression in the dolphin's eyes, as though it hurt to be around me.

Yeah, sorry about that. I heard you guys don't particularly like us. Have you seen an actual human, though? You, know—with two legs? Just now? I rang.

No humans, the dolphin replied. *One ocean human.... now two...you...different.*

What did the dolphin mean, two mers? There was me,

of course, and it sounded like he could tell I was different, probably because I wasn't a full-fledged mer, but who was the other one? Did the guy who dove overboard just turn into a mer too? Was he a Webbed One?

Where is he? The other ocean human? I asked.

But just as my words rang out, a boat from the marina must have started up because the water vibrated around us and the dolphin took off like a shot.

No, wait a second! I tried to swim after the dolphin but it was too fast.

Danger. The dolphin's word rang through the water as it disappeared into the night.

Darn, I rang to no one in particular. Now I was stuck underwater as a mermaid with more questions than ever. Who was the other mer the dolphin was talking about? And why were mers popping up off the coast of the Bahamas where there hadn't been any before? And did this have anything to do with Dillon?

One thing was for sure—I had to find my way back to Cori, Luke, and Trey before they went to get Mom and Dad, or I'd be in a world of trouble. I'd been underwater for about half an hour by then and figured the gang would probably be getting worried.

I swam back to the safety of the docks of the marina and tried to find the jetty with the boat where I'd dived in. All the jetties looked kind of the same so I followed a row of boats until I found an empty berth with a ladder I could climb.

"Guys?" I called out as I surfaced. The warm evening air burned my throat, and my baggy T-shirt billowed around me in the water as I sucked in several deep breaths. Turning *into* a mermaid was fairly fast and painless, but turning back into a human was slower and involved a fair amount of pain. I only came out of the water waist deep, keeping my tail submerged. It was only a matter of a few minutes before my tail started to grow hot, and I braced myself for the intense pain of the change back to legs and feet and toes.

"Jade?" I heard Cori call out in the distance. She sounded like she was a jetty or so over. "Jade, where are you?"

"Over here!" I called out, hoping no one in the nearby boats would hear me and come outside to discover a teenage mermaid in a baggy BAZINGA! T-shirt.

Shots of pain burned through my tail as the scales turned back to skin. By the time the gang reached me a few minutes later, I was in full leg mode.

"There you are," Cori said with a sigh of relief. Trey arrived at her side moments later. "We were dangerously close to getting your mom and dad."

"But you didn't?" I said hopefully.

"No, but I should have. Wasn't this supposed to be a drama-free trip?" Cori asked.

"I'm sorry. I just had to know what was going on with that guy," I said. "Hey, where's Luke?"

"We all split up to try and look for you," Trey said. "He should be around here somewhere. Did you find the guy?"

"No, but I was able to communicate with a dolphin, and get this—one of them said they've seen another ocean human around here," I said.

"A mer, you mean?" Cori asked. "Do you think it was the guy with the hat?"

"Maybe," I replied. "Hey, did you bring my shorts?"

Cori tossed down my shorts so I could get dressed. She tapped Trey on the shoulder and waved her finger for him to turn around.

"Oh, here comes Luke," Trey said as I struggled to pull on the wet shorts.

I could feel the jetty bounce a bit as Luke ran toward us. I finished getting dressed and climbed the ladder with my unsteady legs to get up onto the dock. Luke held out a hand to help me.

"Hey, there. Are you okay?" Luke gave me a hug.

"Yeah, I'm fine," I said, stepping back, "but I'm getting you all wet."

"Don't worry," Luke said, laughing. "Kind of an occupational hazard. Hey, I just saw your guy."

"Where?" I asked as I slipped on my flip-flops, which Cori had brought as well. I squeezed my hair to wring out the water and tried to come up with an excuse for why I was the only one in our group who was soaking wet in case Mom and Dad got suspicious. "I looked everywhere for him."

"Well, I couldn't find Cori and Trey, so I headed back to the original boat where you dove in," Luke replied. "When I got there, I saw the guy climb out of the water and take off."

"Take off how?" I asked, scanning the jetties to see if I could spot him. "Is he still in the marina?"

"No, he rode off in that green speedboat tied up to the yacht," Luke replied.

I remembered the sound of the boat engine that had spooked the dolphins earlier.

"Dillon's speedboat," I said to myself. "Could you tell anything else about him? Like, did he look okay?"

"Yeah, he looked fine," Luke said. "He looked a little hard-core with that goatee and bald head, though."

Bald head? That's when a rush of realization made my head spin and I had to hold on to Luke to keep from losing my balance.

"What's the matter?" Cori asked, catching my arm.

I steadied myself and headed back to Bobbie's sailboat.

"I'm not sure yet."

Chapter Fifteen

Y OU'RE SURE HE WAS bald?" I asked Luke as we hurried along the main trunk of the docks and searched
for the berth with Bobbie's sailboat.

"Yeah, why?" Luke replied.

I undid my ponytail as we walked and tried to braid
my hair into something semi-presentable so it didn't
look like I'd just been on an underwater caper. I couldn't
do anything about my wet clothes, though. I just hoped
the warm evening air had started drying them or that the
cover of darkness would hide my secret once we met up
with our parents.

"I'm just trying to put this all together," I said,
remembering how I'd spotted a man in the porthole of
the Wonderment cruise ship. It had been so far away
that the only thing I could make out was the sun shining off the man's bald head. But he'd had binoculars
focused on me, so I'd turned away before getting a good
look at him.

"Put *what* together?" Cori asked.

"That goateed guy—the bald guy—I think he could be
the same guy I saw throwing something overboard from
that cruise ship," I said.

"Throwing a *dead body* overboard, you mean?" Trey asked in a deep, ominous voice.

"Not this again," Cori said. "Don't you remember? Rayelle's mom says that Dillon guy is bad news. He just planted those ideas in your head. You do have a bit of an overactive imagination after the summer you just had."

"Yeah, I know. But one way or another, something fishy is going on around here," I said.

By then, we'd reached Bobbie's boat, and Mom, Dad, and the Martins were saying their good-byes. I stuck to the shadows to try and hide the fact I'd just spent the last half hour in the water talking to a couple of dolphins.

"Did you kids have fun?" Mom asked as we headed to the gate of the marina. "We were starting to worry."

The lights of the marina cast dark shadows all around us. Could Mom tell my hair and clothes were wet? What would she say if she knew what I'd been up to?

"Yeah," I said. "We got a little sidetracked with all the docks and everything."

"It probably looks a lot different during the day," Mom said.

She had a point. The marina was probably a lot less confusing in the daytime. Could the same be said about what I'd just seen and heard moments earlier with the dolphins and the man in the Wonderment baseball cap? Would the whole situation look different tomorrow once I'd had a chance to sleep on it?

Two cabs were waiting at the gatehouse, one going to the Eutopia, the other going to the Asylum. Trey and Cori exchanged an awkward hug before going to their respective cabs, and Luke pulled me aside to say goodnight under the very watchful eye of my overprotective dad.

"So," he said with a whisper, "I'm not going to try anything with your dad watching me like I was some kind of stalker, but I still owe you that moonlit kiss."

"I'm going to hold you to that," I replied, shivers running down my arms.

Luke waved good-bye and got in his cab, along with Trey and his parents, and we got in the cab behind theirs.

"So, kiddo, have a good night?" Dad asked as he sat next to me and put his arm around me. He hesitated for a second. "Is your hair wet? How did you get your hair wet?"

Darn. I tugged my braid to the other side of my neck. "I either dove underwater back at the marina and had a conversation with a dolphin, or I didn't dry my hair after we went tubing at Teen Club."

Dad let me rest my head on his shoulder. "For my own sanity and your ability to live another day, I'm going to go with the tubing explanation," he said.

"Good plan," I replied.

Cori and I conked out as soon as we got back to the hotel and dragged ourselves out of bed at eleven on Friday morning, just in time to grab showers and hobble down to the dining room. Lunch at the Asylum was the omelet bar, so Cori and I sidled up to the omelet station where a chef with a big white hat was taking orders.

"Man, oh man," I said with a big yawn. "I can't believe my parents' wedding is tomorrow and we have less than forty-eight hours left of this vacation."

"Tell me about it. It's gone by so fast," Cori agreed.

It was my turn to order. "Ham, peppers, onions, and cheese, please. Lots and lots of cheese."

"Make that two," Cori added.

The chef poured olive oil into two of the three skillets in front of him and tossed in the ingredients. Soon a delicious aroma filled the air, making my stomach grumble. He finished a third omelet for the customer in front of us and slid it onto a plate for him.

"That looks so good." My mouth watered at the thought of a warm cheesy omelet, and I was relieved to finally get a decent meal from the Asylum kitchen. I gazed out the long bank of windows overlooking the Caribbean Sea. Seagulls hovered over the water and dipped into the ocean while the wind whipped the fronds of the palm trees. Mom had been right. Things did look a lot different in the bright light of day.

That bald guy from the night before was probably up to no good, but that didn't mean he had anything to do with anything else.

"So tomorrow's the big day," Cori said. "You excited?"

I searched for Mom and Dad in the dining room and caught them holding hands at a table out on the balcony.

"Yeah," I said. "If someone actually shows up to marry the happy couple, we'll be golden."

"And if my mom and dad arrive on time," Cori said, looking at her watch.

"What time is their flight again?" I asked, remembering that Mr. and Mrs. Blake should be flying in later that day.

"Not sure. I haven't been able to email them since my phone died," Cori said.

"You should have told me!" I replied. "I could have loaned you mine."

Just as I took my phone out of my bag, it buzzed with a new email. That's when it occurred to me—I never did email Rayelle back after I'd told her what Kiki's boyfriend said. I'd forgotten my phone at the hotel yesterday morning then had gotten home so late from the marina that I'd completely blanked on getting back to her.

"Oh, shoot," I said, looking at her name on my phone's screen.

"Avoiding a Martin brother too, are you?" Cori said, nodding to my phone.

"No, it's not that," I said, tapping on the email to read her message. "It's just Rayelle. Probably about Dillon."

Cori rolled her eyes. "Hopefully she's heard back from that officer guy."

Of course. Officer Ensel had probably sorted it all out and Rayelle wanted to let me know.

Hi Jade,

Dillon's mom just called my mom saying she still hasn't heard from him and is getting worried. Just wondering if your parents had any ideas after all because there is still no sign of him on this end.

—Rayelle

"Huh," I said, staring at the screen. "She says Dillon's mom just called and he's still missing."

"Pepper?" the chef asked.

"Um, pardon me?" I asked, trying to understand what he meant.

"For your omelet," Cori whispered.

"Oh, no thanks," I said as I took my plate. Cori's omelet was done seconds later, so we went outside to join Mom and Dad at their table where they were enjoying their post-lunch coffees.

"Hey, guys," I said as I sat down.

"Finally decided to grace us with your presence?" Dad teased.

"Dalrymple, they're teenagers after all," Mom said. "I'm impressed we've gotten them out of bed before ten at all this week."

"Thanks, Mom. I think," I said with a laugh then turned to Dad. "Hey, did that officer ever call back about Dillon?"

"There was a message from Officer Ensel when we

got back to the hotel last night saying not to worry. Dillon is back home safe and sound with his family," Dad said. "Apparently he was just staying with a friend for a couple days and didn't think to call his mother. So, mystery solved."

Cori and I exchanged confused looks. If Dillon was back home, why was his mom still calling to find out where he was?

"I also just got a text from your mom, Cori," Mom said, beaming. "They're heading out to the airport to catch their flight, which means everyone will finally be here soon."

Mom's smile was so big that I hated to crush her happiness with more worries about this Dillon business. I needed to find out more information before I bothered her with it. But how, exactly, was I supposed to do that?

"That's exciting," I said, continuing our conversation about the wedding. "I know how much you wanted Mrs. Blake here. But are you going to be okay even if this wedding doesn't turn out the way you expected it to?"

"Well, that's another piece of good news," Dad said. "Town Hall called to say someone came into their office this week to renew their officiate papers. If they can get the paperwork through by the end of the day, we may have someone to perform the ceremony after all."

"Wow!" I exclaimed. "That's amazing!"

"Now don't get too excited. They still need to process the paperwork, so nothing is for sure yet." Dad reached for Mom's hand and kissed it.

"So what's the plan for the rest of the day?" I asked as the news about Officer Ensel's call preyed on my mind.

I tried to arrange all the pieces of the Dillon puzzle together: the body (or whatever it was!) Dillon and I saw being thrown out of the Wonderment cruise ship's porthole, Dillon's speedboat abandoned near the same ship, the "W" hat dude talking to Officer Ensel at the Straw Market, the same "W" hat on the goateed, bald man from the marina who took off in Dillon's boat. How did they all fit together?

Could the answer to the Dillon mystery be found on the Wonderment cruise ship?

"Cori's parents won't arrive in time for dinner, but we're planning to meet them at the comedy club near the pier after that," Mom said.

"Oh, I should go call the restaurant to make sure they have our reservation all set," Dad said, excusing himself from the table to go back up to their room for the restaurant's phone number.

"All of us are going to the comedy club, then?" I asked, taking another bite of my omelet.

"Yes, the Martins, the Blakes, Bobbie and Eddie—"

"Mom," I interrupted, trying to come up with a way to get onto the Wonderment cruise ship so we could solve the Dillon mystery once and for all. "We were talking to some kids from Teen Club, and a few of them are going to that Taylor 'n Tyler concert."

Cori looked at me from across the table and shrugged as

if wondering what the heck I was saying. And she was right. The concert on the Wonderment cruise ship was supposed to be for the kids in the Sparkle Wish Club. How were we supposed to swing that?

"And you were thinking a pop concert might be more interesting than a washed-up comedian from a ten-year-old sitcom?" Mom asked, eyebrow raised.

"Kinda?" I said.

"Oh, all right," Mom said with a smile. "Find out about tickets, and I'll talk to your dad. We're going to go back upstairs to rest before everyone arrives. You girls let us know when you get back to the room, okay?"

"Will do!" I said cheerily as Mom left the table.

"That was *weird*," Cori said once Mom was gone. "Why would Officer Ensel say Dillon was back home if it wasn't true? Something is *not* right about this whole Dillon business."

"Finally!" I exclaimed. "Someone believes me."

"Kind of what Dillon's been hoping for all this time, huh?" Cori asked.

"Exactly," I agreed, feeling guiltier than ever for not backing Dillon up at the Straw Market on Monday when he said he saw a body being tossed from the porthole. "I'm going to email Rayelle to give her a heads-up." I pulled out my phone and emailed her to let her in on the plan and made sure to memorize her email address this time, just in case. "Meanwhile, we *have* to get on that ship and see what's up with that bald guy. I have a feeling he didn't just find Dillon's boat by accident."

"You know that concert is closed to the general public, right?" Cori asked.

"Yes, but if we don't find out what's really going on, we'll never know what happened to Dillon. We need to get tickets for that concert," I said.

Cori stared off over the ocean for a second then seemed to get an idea.

"Do you still have that Taylor 'n Tyler autograph?" she asked.

I wasn't sure what she was planning, but I hunted through my bag and found the autograph among Faye's and Officer Ensel's business cards.

"Right here," I said, producing the slip of paper with the autograph. Cori took it from me, opened up the paper, and smiled.

"Don't worry about tickets. I'll hook you up," she said.

THANKFULLY, MACY AND NICK were happy to trade their extra Taylor 'n Tyler tickets for a personalized autograph, so things were starting to come together.

That night, we had an early dinner with the Martins at a diner by the pier, so that afterward we could walk to the concert at the Wonderment cruise ship, which was docked a half mile or so away.

"Oh, before I forget—here," Cori said as our parents went to pay the bill. She hunted in her bag and pulled out three badges on strings and handed them to Luke, Trey, and me.

"What are these?" I asked, but I had a feeling I should know since the string looked so familiar.

"The Taylor 'n Tyler ticket passes," Cori replied.

I studied the passes. The cards had the concert information along with a Wonderment Cruiselines emblem and a black magnetic strip on the back.

"What's with the strip thingy?" I asked.

"It's a security thing. We probably need to swipe the cards to get on the ship," Cori replied. "We had the same kind of passes on our Alaskan cruise."

"Oh!" I said in realization, dangling the pass from its neon blue string. "This is so weird!"

"What?" Luke asked.

"The string on this badge," I said, holding it up. "It's the same type of string I found in Dillon's speedboat at the shipyard the other day. Look—" I showed Cori— "it has the same metal clip."

"Why would Dillon have a string from a Taylor 'n Tyler concert pass?" Luke asked.

"Not a concert pass but maybe he has a ship pass," I said. "Cori, you heard Kiki say how badly he wanted to get on the ship. What if he swiped a pass from someone?"

"Rayelle's mom *did* say he got caught pickpocketing at the market once," Cori said thoughtfully.

"Yeah, but it doesn't take four days to look around a ship," Luke said. "So, why is he still missing? That doesn't make any sense."

"Nothing about this situation makes sense—all the more reason to get on that ship to see what the heck is going on," I said, stashing the concert pass in my bag.

"Then let's bounce," Trey said.

We joined our parents at the cash register to say good-bye.

"Say hi to my mom and dad when you guys meet up at the comedy club," Cori said.

"We will, sweetie," Mom said. "You guys have fun but be careful."

"Don't worry," I said. "Between two fourteen-year-olds, a fifteen-year-old, and a sixteen-year-old, it's like we're practically as responsible as a senior citizen."

"Hey, don't let Gran hear you say that!" Dad said with a laugh.

"Here, take my phone and stick together," Mr. Martin said. He reached into his pocket and handed his phone to Trey. "We'll come meet you in a cab once the concert's done, but call if you need anything."

We said our good-byes and headed down the waterfront to where the Wonderment cruise ship was docked. I wasn't sure what we'd find out about Dillon once we got there, maybe nothing, but all the clues we had so far pointed to that ship.

Along the way, Cori kept dropping hints to Trey about how Taylor 'n Tyler did the soundtrack to an upcoming romantic comedy, but he was engrossed in a game of Angry Birds on his dad's phone.

"So, I was thinking maybe we could all go to the movie when we get back home," Cori said.

"Ohhhh! That was close!" Trey exclaimed, staring at the phone's screen.

"That's *it*." Cori stopped dead in her tracks.

"What?" Trey asked, looking up from the phone to see what was going on.

Luke and I glanced at each other, preparing ourselves for whatever wrath Cori was about to unleash on Trey.

"First you ruin a perfect moonlit walk on the beach, then you wreck a potentially romantic stroll around the marina, and now you can't stop playing on that stupid phone long enough to have a normal conversation with your girlfriend?" Cori asked.

"But—" Trey started, looking completely confused.

"You, Trey Martin, have no clue when it comes to being a boyfriend. Right, Jade?" She turned to me.

I cringed, not knowing what to do.

Trey finally found his voice.

"Well, maybe your definition of 'boyfriend' is a little whacked," he said.

"Whacked? Is it whacked to want a little romance?" Cori asked, her eyes welling with tears as she stalked away.

I dropped Luke's hand and jogged ahead to Cori's side to put an arm around her.

Trey called after her. "Not when 'romance' means comparing me to all those guys in your teen magazines." I looked over my shoulder and saw him turn to Luke. "Back me up here, bro!"

Luke looked from me to Trey.

"Come on," Luke said, slapping his brother on the back. "Let's just get to the concert."

We walked in silence for a while, with Cori and I up ahead and Luke and Trey lingering behind. If this was how it was going to be with Trey and Cori, what did that mean for Luke and me? I could see Cori's point, but was it fair to fault Trey for just being Trey? Was there a right and a wrong side to all this?

We were almost at the ship and I could hear music pumping from the upper deck, making my ears ring. Or was that another kind of ring?

Help…

I spun around, looking to see if Luke was talking to me, but his face was just as confused as I felt.

Help...

"Are those the dolphins again?" I asked Luke.

"I'm not sure," Luke said.

"What are you guys talking about?" Cori asked.

"A ringing sound," I said, straining to hear.

"Don't forget us mere mortals," Trey joked. "You mind clueing us in?"

I looked around to make sure it was safe to speak. A couple strolled a few dozen feet ahead and a family with a dog played in a nearby park with their backs turned to us, but other than that, the coast was clear.

"Luke and I can hear something calling for help in the water down there." I looked into the harbor to see if I could spot anything. There were no signs of dolphins as far as I could tell, yet the ringing continued. I turned to the others.

"You're getting that look in your eyes again," Luke said.

He was right. It was like one of those ancient mer laws that forced mers to help people in need, but this time it wasn't a human who needed me. Was it a dolphin? Another mer? Something else? I had to find out what was happening down there and see if I could help. "There's something wrong."

I looked along the dock for a place to climb down into the water then ran toward a ladder.

"Jade!" Cori called after me. "Not this again. You can't go chasing after every stray dolphin in the ocean."

"That's just it," I said as I flicked off my flip-flops, ditched my bag, and made my way down the ladder into the water. Thankfully, I'd worn a sundress with pockets, so I disrobed from the waist down and slipped my unmentionables in my pocket before anyone could notice what I was doing. "I'm not sure this is a dolphin."

"Okay, okay. I'll hold your bag," Cori said, clutching it to her chest.

"And we'll be your lookouts," Luke said as he and Trey sat on the side of the pier, their backs to the pillar.

"Thanks, guys."

I dove into the water and tried to sense the sound, but I couldn't hear the ringing just then. After a couple of deep breaths of water, I was tail-ified and swimming deep into the harbor to see what I could see.

Help, the voice came again. It was definitely not a dolphin.

Hello? I called out, trying to swim in the direction of the sound.

Then I saw him a few dozen feet underwater. A mer about Dad's age at the base of one of the dock's vertical pillars, with a green backpack at his side.

I could hear several dolphins now, off in the distance. They were staying away, probably because of the double whammy of mers in their midst. This was the other mer the dolphin had talked about the night before! It had to be.

Are you okay? I said as I reached him.

Who...who's there? Where did you come from? The mer blinked quickly and stared past me through the water.

My name is Jade. Is there something wrong with your eyes? I asked.

I can't see you. His face creased into a pained expression.

You're blind? I asked. *How can you survive underwater if you can't see?*

My sight has been getting worse and worse since I was forced underwater with this thing. He reached out and searched through the water until his hand rested on the backpack beside him. *At first, I could see in shadows but now everything is dark.*

What do you mean? Who forced you underwater? I asked. Whoever it was, it must be a human to have access to a backpack. The mer uttered the next few words in low, garbled rings, as if trying to make sense of his situation.

No hair. He let go of the backpack and touched his face. *Goatee.*

Bald with a goatee. The guy we saw at the marina?

Wait a second, how do you know the word "goatee"? I rang to the merman. That's when I noticed he didn't have long hair and a beard like all the other mermen I knew. *Are you a Webbed One?*

Yes. My name is Henry. The merman forced out the next few sentences. *That bald man found out my secret back in Florida and kidnapped me. He forced me onto a ship and threatened to hurt my family unless I helped him smuggle this bag onto the island.*

How long have you been underwater like this? I asked.

Four days, I think, Henry replied. *It feels like forever.*

I did the reverse engineering on that and realized Henry had been stuck underwater since Monday. The same day we arrived in the Bahamas and I met Dillon at the Straw Market. My mind worked to connect the dots on everything that must have happened since then.

Did this guy toss you into the water from the ship's porthole? I asked on a hunch.

Henry nodded.

So, that body Dillon and I saw being thrown overboard from the cruise ship wasn't a body at all. It was a mer! A mer with a backpack.

I was supposed to deliver this backpack to a yellow hook below a place called Señor Frog's so the bald guy's customer could pick it up, Henry rang, rubbing his eyes. *But as soon as I hit the water, my eyesight went bad and I couldn't find the drop-off.*

He explained how the blindness was the reason he became a Webbed One in the first place. It reminded me of how my old boss Bridget was given Land Status because of a tail condition called scaliosis. She couldn't survive in the ocean as a mer because her tail would swell to the point that she couldn't swim.

I'm supposed to meet the bald man at the marina once I make the delivery, so he can take me back to my family in Florida, but I can't find the marina either. Henry blinked again. *I've been staying close to the ship ever since, so I don't get lost.*

So Baldie from the marina and Baldie from the porthole *were* the same guy. And that's why he'd been at the marina the night before. He was looking for Henry, trying to figure out what happened to his package.

I thought for sure he was leaving me behind when the ship left port the other day, so I tried to follow it back to Florida when I could at least see shadows, but it only led me back here, Henry continued. *Now I can't see anything.*

My mind suddenly flashed to earlier that week when we were Snuba diving and saw a lone scuba diver with the green oxygen tank on his back off in the distance. It had not been a scuba diver after all! It was a merman with a green backpack.

What's in this thing, anyway? I unzipped the backpack. It was hard to see in the dim light but inside was a bunch of colorful packages wrapped in sealed plastic.

I have no idea, but if I don't deliver it to the bald guy's customer, I'll never get home, Henry said.

I think I can help you. I have some friends up on the pier. Luke! I rang but I could hear the music getting louder, and I wasn't sure if he could hear me.

Who are you calling? Henry asked, waving his head back and forth but still unable to see. *You're the only other mer I've come across since I got here. Did you dive into the water to save me? Are you a Webbed One too?*

Kind of, I rang back. *My mom's a mermaid and my dad's human so I get to trade in my tail for legs a lot easier than most mers. Wait here.*

I swam up to the surface and called out to the gang back on the pier. "Hey, guys!"

"Shh!" Cori brought a finger to her lips and whispered down to me. "There are people around."

Luke, can you hear me? I rang in my mer voice as Cori winced at the high-pitched ring.

What did you find? Luke asked, peering down into the water.

A mer is in trouble down here. He's the guy who got tossed overboard from the cruise ship. Can you guys call your grandpa so he and Bobbie can help him?

We're on it! Luke motioned to Trey for the phone so he could make the call.

I dove back down into the water to catch my breath and check on Henry. He had pulled the backpack onto his back.

Wait! I called out. *Where are you going with that?*

I was hoping you could help me get it to Señor Frog's before the ship leaves again, Henry rang.

Forget about the bag. I explained about Eddie and Bobbie and how they could help him turn back into a human once they got him back to Florida.

But if that bald guy finds out I ditched his stuff and escaped, he'll just come looking for me in Florida. He told me he'd hurt my kids.

You have kids? I asked. In all my time as a mermaid, I'd never met anyone else like me. Someone who was part mer and part human. And now Baldie was threatening them?

Yeah, Alex and Amanda. Henry's pained expression softened. *They're twins. So I really need to deliver this thing.*

The only thing you're going to do is wait here for Bobbie and Eddie to come so they can help you. As far as the backpack? Just leave that part to me.

Chapter Seventeen

I WASN'T EXACTLY SURE HOW I was going to deliver the backpack like I'd promised Henry, but I picked up the heavy bag from the ocean floor and hooked it onto a spike partway up the pier's pillar before I got out of the water. That way, I could find it again when I had the chance. First, though, I had to get on the cruise ship to figure out if there was a connection between Baldie and Dillon.

If Dillon had a ship pass, was he onboard? Had he been there all week? Was something (or somebody!) keeping him there? I *had* to find out. Kidnapping, smuggling… what else was Baldie capable of? Would he hurt Dillon if he caught him poking around?

Cori and Trey stayed behind to show Bobbie and Eddie where to find Henry once they got there with the sailboat. I'd told Henry to hang out by the surface of the water so he could hear Bobbie and let her lead him back to the shelter of the marina, where she and Eddie could help him.

Meanwhile, Luke and I continued to the cruise ship.

We stood with a group of spectators with Sparkle Wish T-shirts as they milled around the dock, waiting to board the Wonderment cruise ship for the Taylor 'n Tyler concert. An awkward silence stretched between us, neither of us sure how to act after being put in the middle of Trey and Cori's fight earlier. I figured I could kiss that moonlit kiss good-bye.

"So..." I began, trying to break the ice. "How are we going to find our way around once we get in there?"

"I dunno. But are you sure we should do this? This bald guy sounds kinda dangerous," Luke said. "Besides, how do we even know this Dillon guy is here?"

"We don't," I replied as I strung the concert pass around my neck. "That's what we're here to find out."

"Either way, maybe we should call the police," Luke suggested.

"And tell them what?" I asked. "Like you said, we have no idea if Dillon is actually here."

"Well, isn't this bald guy trying to smuggle something onto the island? I'm sure that's something the cops would like to know."

"Think about it," I said. "How do we explain that we know that? A guy with the tail of a fish told us?"

"Good point," Luke said. "But we should at least call our parents."

"Let's just check things out first," I suggested. "If something's up, I'll be the first to dial the number. But if this turns out to be nothing, all the better. Then my parents can keep enjoying a night out with all their closest friends before their wedding day. Deal?"

"All right. Deal," Luke agreed reluctantly.

"Now we just have to find our way around," I said.

"Good news." Luke pulled out his dad's cell phone. "We have the power of Google on our side. Plus now Cori won't end up pushing Trey into the harbor for playing Angry Birds."

"Win-win," I replied.

"What do you need to know?" Luke asked, his finger poised over the phone's screen.

"Maybe you can pull up some information on this particular ship so we know what we're dealing with," I suggested.

"Already on it," Luke said, scrolling through his search results.

"I overheard one of the organizers say the concert is on the upper deck," I said. "We know that at least."

"And it looks like there are two rows of portholes and three decks with balconies as far as I can tell, so six decks in all," Luke said.

I scanned the ship to try to find the porthole where I'd seen the bald man throw Henry overboard.

"The porthole where we saw Henry being dumped is on the other side of the ship," I replied.

"That might be worth a stop on our tour," Luke said.

"Definitely," I replied.

A dozen or so Sparkle Wish organizers herded us all behind a roped-off area, and minutes later, several policemen arrived in cruisers, accompanying a long, black limousine.

"That's them!" one of the girls from our group yelled. Sure enough, Taylor 'n Tyler emerged from the back of the limousine, flanked by bodyguards. They turned toward the crowd and waved, flashing their bright white smiles as a group of paparazzi jostled to get a good picture while the police officers managed the crowds behind the rope barriers. After several minutes of posing and waving, Taylor 'n Tyler disappeared up the gangplank to head to the concert on the upper deck.

"Hey, maybe Officer Ensel is on duty here," Luke said. "Maybe he can clear this whole thing up."

I searched each officer's face, but none of them was Ensel. "No, none of these guys look familiar."

"But one of them might know about Dillon's case at least," Luke said. "It wouldn't hurt to check."

"Good point. Excuse me!" I called out. A lady cop was adjusting the barriers a little farther along the crowd. She looked my way.

"Can I help you?" she asked.

"Sorry to bother you, but we're wondering about a friend who went missing this week. We had been dealing with Officer Ensel. He told us our friend Dillon had been found, but his mother is still looking for him. I'm sorry I don't know Dillon's last name, we only just met, but we were wondering if you knew where he was."

The officer looked at me skeptically. "Who was the officer you spoke to again?"

"Ensel," I replied.

"Carl Ensel?" she asked. "I work at his precinct, and there have been no missing person reports this week."

"That's weird," Luke said.

The officer asked me for a few more details about Dillon. She wrote something in her notepad and put it back in her pocket then pulled out a card similar to Officer Ensel's. "I'll look into this, but if you have any other information, please give me a call."

"Thanks," I said, tucking the card in my bag. I secretly wondered if anyone was actually interested in looking for Dillon. Ensel didn't seem to be. Kiki and her boyfriend thought he'd just taken off somewhere, and his own mother had taken three days to start getting concerned.

I looked at Luke with raised eyebrows once the officer moved on. But by then, the guides from the Sparkle Wish Club and ship staff had started to lead the spectators up the gangplank onto the ship, so there was no time to talk. Everyone had to swipe their passcards to get on the ship, just like Cori had predicted.

"Please keep the passcard visible at all times and stay with the group," a Sparkle Wish guide announced.

The hallway leading to the elevators and stairs was jam-packed and Luke reached for my hand. Did that mean we were okay despite what had just happened with Cori and Trey?

We'd finally gotten past the worst of the crowd and reached a landing with a bank of elevators when Luke dropped my hand again.

"That was weird with that officer, right?" I asked, trying not to overanalyze the whole hand-holding thing. Oh, who was I kidding? I kept right on overanalyzing the whole hand-holding thing!

"I know. It doesn't sound like this Ensel guy even looked into Dillon's disappearance," Luke whispered.

"Officer Ensel told my dad he would try to be discreet. Maybe he kept Dillon's case off the books as a favor." I was seriously starting to wonder whether we were on a wild-goose chase.

"So should we just drop it?" Luke asked.

"No!" I replied louder than I'd intended. Something just kept nagging at me about the whole situation.

"Didn't think so," Luke said with a wry smile.

"I mean, we're here already," I replied, a bit less force-fully. "It wouldn't hurt to take a look around."

"Do we try to find out about the porthole first?" Luke asked.

"That depends. How far can we get with these pass cards?" I looked at the cruise-ship staff and some of the pas-sengers trying to get through the crowd of newcomers. They all had plastic cards on strings hanging from their necks too.

"Ours won't get us into private cabins or anything, but now that we're on board, we should be able to get to all the public areas. We probably don't want to make it too obvious that we're snooping around though."

I considered this for a second.

"Let's go to the upper deck where the concert is sup-posed to be to make it look like we're part of the crowd, then slip out once the concert gets started so we can get the lay of the land," I said.

The elevators were taking forever and several of the Sparkle Wishers were in wheelchairs, so we headed up the stairs. By the fourth floor, I thought I was going to puke.

"How big is this ship, anyway?"

"Come on. Just two more floors." Luke laughed, grabbing my arm.

We made it up the last few steps and rested on the upper deck, leaning on the railing over the water. The concert was being held in the middle of the ship, where they had one of the swimming pools covered with a platform for the spectators and a higher platform tricked out with instruments, microphones, and stage lights. Large video screens were already showing one of Taylor 'n Tyler's latest music videos, and the air all around the ship seemed to sparkle with excitement.

Kids streamed past us and headed down to mid-deck to find a spot to view the concert.

I braced my elbows on the ship's railing and looked overboard. I could see the balconies' white railings tucked into the side of the ship for a few decks down, but it was hard to see the portholes from that angle.

"The porthole I saw was way at the back," I said. "But you can't see it from here, especially with the way the ship curves toward the stern."

"Perfect for tossing mers overboard," Luke said.

"Mers with two-ton backpacks," I added.

"I forgot to ask. What was in that backpack, anyway?" Luke asked.

I thought back to how Bobbie and Eddie had stopped those drug smugglers off the coast of Florida and got a sick feeling in the pit of my stomach. "I don't know, but I'm thinking they weren't Mickey Mouse watches."

Suddenly, the music from the stage pumped up and a group of very enthusiastic cruise-ship employees jumped onto the stage and started dancing and clapping.

"Hi, everyone!" a cheery girl in a cruise ship T-shirt called out to the audience. "Welcome to Taylor 'n Tyler's benefit concert for the Sparkle Wish Club. Wonderment Cruiselines has made a donation on behalf of all our crew, and Taylor 'n Tyler are not only here tonight to entertain everyone but have generously matched our donation as well, so more Sparkle Wishers can be granted their wishes!"

A huge cheer rose from the audience. It made me think of how Cori and I had been so annoyed when we thought Taylor 'n Tyler bumped our reservation at the Eutopia. Now, I felt completely horrible, since they were obviously really good guys doing a very good thing for a worthy charity.

"And now, without further ado, here are Taylor 'n Tyler!"

Another huge cheer erupted, and Luke and I were jostled between enthusiastic fans.

This is crazy, I rang to Luke in my mer voice so he could understand me over the noise.

And pretty cool. Look! He pointed to where Taylor 'n Tyler had taken to the stage. They sang and danced to their new single, sending the fans into a frenzy.

Once the concert was in full swing, Luke grabbed

my hand again (good sign!) and we casually made our way through the crowd to the edge of the deck where he dropped it again (bad sign!), so we could slip back to the stairwell to try and make it to the floor with the porthole. The sun had set by then and it was nearly dark.

"Can you get your grandpa on the phone again?" I asked Luke once we were safely in the stairwell. "If he and Bobbie have Henry, we could find out a bit more about this Baldie guy."

"Good idea." Luke took out the phone and pressed redial then handed the phone to me.

"Hello?" Eddie answered and passed me off to Bobbie.

"Hi, Bobbie, it's Jade. Did you find Henry?" I asked.

"Yes, he's here with us at the marina. Should I call your parents? Where are you?"

I wasn't sure what to say. Mom and Dad were getting married the next day. At least I hoped they were. The whole thing with Henry was handled as far as I was concerned. I just wanted to see if there was any evidence that Dillon was indeed on the ship. If so, I promised myself I would call the police and my parents right away. Baldie had already proven to be a very bad dude, and I had no intention of coming face to face with the guy.

"Oh, no. No need to call my parents but if you see them just tell them Luke and I didn't want to miss the concert so we're on the cruise ship like we'd planned."

"Trey and Cori should be there soon," Bobbie said. "They've got my phone if you need them."

She told me the number so Luke could program it into his dad's phone.

"Good, thanks. I was also wondering if you could ask Henry a few questions. I'm curious if he knows anything else about the bald guy who did this to him. Like what part of the ship does he work in?" I asked.

"Just a second," Bobbie said, and I could tell by the ring through the phone that she was asking him. I waited a few moments, then Bobbie came back on the phone. I tilted the phone a little so Luke could listen in. "He says the bald man got him on the ship in a shipping container through the loading dock then transported him in a maintenance cart to a room with a porthole. Henry was kept tied up and gagged, but he heard the man call his boss to tell him he was closing part of that deck for maintenance."

So that's how Baldie got away with holding someone hostage on the ship all the way from Florida.

"Does Henry know what room it was?" I asked and waited the few moments it took for Bobbie to ask the question.

"He says 1078," Bobbie replied. "The phone in the room was disconnected but that's what the display on the handset said. But why do you want to know? I don't want you kids to do anything silly. That man is obviously dangerous."

"It would be good to know so we can tell the cops if there's any way to get this guy in trouble."

"Unfortunately it will be really hard to do that since

there are mers involved. Not exactly the kind of evidence we want to turn over to the police," Bobbie replied.

That was true, just like I'd told Luke. But I had a feeling there might be something else we could pin on Baldie. A way to make sure he never bothered Henry again. And if my hunch was right, it might mean helping someone else in trouble.

"You're right. Okay, thanks," I replied and hung up.

"So what's next?" Luke asked.

"More stairs?"

"Let's do it."

L UKE AND I HOOFED it downstairs. The landing on the first floor opened into two hallways, and we went the wrong way at first but then got ourselves turned around and headed in the right direction toward 1078. We could only get as far as cabin 1070 where part of the hallway was blocked off with yellow tape. A sign hung from the tape: "Electrical Work in Progress. This Area Closed."

"Electrical work, yeah right," I said to Luke and we ducked under the tape. Cabin 1078 was the last room at the end of the hallway. I knocked on the door.

"Are you crazy?" Luke whispered behind me. "What if he's in there?"

"Isn't that why we're here? To find out?" I asked, not quite understanding what Luke meant.

"Jade, this guy is dangerous," Luke said. "You saw what he did to Henry."

"Not Baldie," I replied. "I'm talking about Dillon."

But Luke had a point. What if the door opened and I came face to face with a mer-kidnapping smuggler? I'd come too far to turn back now, though, so I put my ear to the door, ready to run for my life if necessary. There were thudding sounds from inside, like someone was trying to send a message.

"Dillon?" I whispered as loudly as I dared. "If you can hear me, knock three times."

I waited a few seconds, and sure enough, three knocks sounded from inside the room. My heart seized in my chest. How long had Dillon been held captive in this room? I wondered. How scared had he been all this time?

"Don't worry, Dillon. We're going to call for help," I whispered back. "Hang in there."

I hadn't stuck up for Dillon that day back at the Straw Market and look where that got him. I had to make this right. But rescuing a prisoner from a locked room was beyond my skill set. It was time to get the police involved.

"Do we call 911?" Luke asked, pulling out his phone.

"I'm not sure if 911 works in the Bahamas." I slid off my backpack and pulled out the lady officer's card. "Here, try this number."

Luke took the card and held up his dad's phone, looking for reception. "I can't get a signal down here. We're going to have to go back to the upper deck."

"We can't just leave him here," I said, looking at the door and wondering if Dillon was hurt. "You go and I'll stay."

"Forget it," Luke said. "There's no way I'm leaving you down here by yourself."

The decision was made for us when the door to a maintenance room a few feet away creaked open. We hustled down the hallway and ducked under the yellow tape.

"Hey!" I heard a booming voice and stole a quick glance

over my shoulder. I couldn't get a good look at the guy, but he had a blue Wonderment Cruiselines hat on. "Hey, you two!" he called again, sending a shudder of fear through my body.

"Go, go, go!" I said to Luke. We ran to the stairwell and started back up the stairs. "We can get lost in the concert crowd."

Gah! So many stairs!

I thought I was going to lose my lunch by the time we reached the top floor but thankfully, it didn't seem like the guy was following us because I couldn't hear his footfalls on the stairs. By then, Luke had gotten reception on the cell phone and was dialing the lady officer's number. He explained who we were and that we'd found Dillon.

"Our friend is being held in cabin 1078, but hurry! We think the man who's been holding him captive is after us," Luke said.

"Do you really think that was him?" I whispered. "Maybe it was just some other maintenance worker."

No sooner were the words out of my mouth than the elevator doors slid open and a goateed, ball-capped man stepped out.

"You're that girl from the marina, aren't ya?" Baldie pulled a large wrench from his pocket and slapped it into the palm of his other hand. "Hasn't anyone ever told you it's not polite to snoop around where you don't—"

We took off before he could finish his sentence.

"This guy's even crazier than Finalin and Medora,"

I called over my shoulder as we ran out onto the upper deck to the blaring music and crushing crowds of the Taylor 'n Tyler concert. I reached behind to grab Luke's hand, remembering the two homicidal mers we'd met in Talisman Lake earlier that year. The only difference was that Finalin and Medora were crazy with a good cause—to free all the mers who'd been wrongfully imprisoned in the lake by the Mermish Council.

Baldie was just a straight-up maniac!

He won't try anything with all these people around, Luke rang to me in his mer voice as we traveled deeper and deeper into the crowd.

I hope not, I rang back, looking around at all the happy fans clapping and singing along to Taylor 'n Tyler's music.

"Hi!" Someone grabbed my arm, nearly scaring me out of my flip-flops. It was Macy, with Nick and their parents. "Are you guys having fun?"

"Oh, hi!" I replied in surprise.

Baldie might not do anything stupid with all these people around, but could I really take that chance? Hadn't Henry said he'd forced him onto the ship? What if he had a gun? That was nothing to mess around with. "We're having a ball. Thanks so much for the tickets."

"Where are your friends?" Macy asked.

"We're actually looking for them right now." I could see that Luke was texting Cori and Trey to let them know what was going on. I caught a glimpse of a blue Wonderment Cruiselines ball cap on the right side of the ship near the railing. "Stick close to your parents, okay? And enjoy the rest of the show."

We have to get out of here. Who knows what this guy is capable of doing. I don't want any of these kids getting hurt, I rang to Luke and pointed to the other side of the ship away from Baldie. *That way.*

Baldie was in the path of the stairs, so we worked our way through the crowd to the bow to hide out until the coast was clear. There was another large swimming pool at the bow with the super-big waterslide that went out and over the water. Just looking at it made my stomach do somersaults.

The pool was closed for the evening, and no one was around since most people were at the concert.

"Let's hide under here," I suggested and led Luke underneath the waterslide where we could take cover until help arrived. Something nagged at me as we waited.

"What I don't get is why go through all the trouble of dumping a merman into the water to do your dirty work?" I whispered. "And then to kidnap Dillon?"

"You saw the security coming in here," Luke said. "There's no way Baldie could have smuggled the bag through there. Plus, I'm pretty sure it would have had to go through customs and that wouldn't have worked out too well for him."

"I bet he never intended to help Henry get home," I said, my body boiling with seething rage aimed at the man in the blue Wonderment Cruiselines baseball cap.

"But now Baldie's in so deep. No wonder he doesn't want Dillon talking," Luke said.

Then it occurred to me. "What if he gets back to 1078 before the cops get there?"

"You're right. I should call that officer again," Luke said.

"Just try to be quiet," I said, peeking over the edge of the pool to see if anyone had followed us.

Luke was on the phone again and I could hear the conversation from his end.

"Uh-huh...yeah, those are our friends...okay, good...thanks for letting us know." Luke hung up and turned to me. "She said they have police on the ship now, and they're going to ring the alarm for everyone to evacuate so they can catch this guy. She's got Cori and Trey with her."

"We should get out of here," I said, starting to stand.

"No wait." Luke pulled me back down. "There's our guy."

There he was all right.

"I don't think he sees us." Baldie stood by the narrow gangway leading to the stairs, underneath a row of hanging lifeboats. He had his back to us and was looking out over the water as he talked on his phone.

"Carl—dude!" Baldie said into his phone. "I know the drop went bad last time with that other scuba diver but this new guy is legit. I'm telling you, man, this guy is the best diver in Florida—the stuff should have been there by now. Are you sure you're looking on the big yellow hook? Off the pier below Señor Frog's?"

Carl? I rang to Luke. *Why does that name sound familiar?* I racked my brain, trying to come up with the answer.

Is it someone you met this week? Luke asked.

I thought back but couldn't make the connection then I nudged Luke. *Can I have the phone?*

I found the phone's email program and hoped I remembered Rayelle's email.

> Hi Rayelle, this is Jade emailing from another phone. Just wanted to let you know we found Dillon and the police have everything under control. PS Do you know anyone named Carl?
>
> —Jade

It only took about two minutes for Rayelle to respond.

> Hooray! I hope he's okay!! PS I'm not sure but isn't Officer Ensel's first name Carl?
>
> —Rayelle

Moments later, the alarm sounded. Baldie looked around, trying to piece together what was happening. He yelled into his phone.

"No! You listen to me, Carl!" Baldie continued. "If you ratted me out to your police friends, I'll be the first one to point the finger back at you. One way or another, you owe me a hundred grand. Either for the goods or my silence."

Police. Carl. Carl Ensel.

Officer Ensel must have been in on this the whole time! I rang to Luke.

That's when I decided that I needed to get evidence to nail Ensel too.

We need to get this on video. I remembered how Cori had recorded Taylor 'n Tyler, trying to get them to confess that they'd stolen our hotel reservation. If we could get Baldie on video talking to Ensel, it would be proof they were in on it together.

Then we had to get out of there—and fast! I held up Mr. Martin's phone. *Do you know how this works?*

Here, Luke said, taking the phone from me. We stayed low and circled around the big pool with the massive waterslide to try and get a little closer. Baldie turned our way but not before we ducked behind the waterslide just in time.

Baldie kept talking into his phone, but we couldn't risk getting video. Luke just tried to record the audio, but I doubted the phone was picking up anything with the sound of the alarm blaring overhead.

Then, all of a sudden, Mr. Martin's phone rang. It was Dad's number. He probably caught wind of what was happening and was freaking. Not the best time to ream me out, Dad!

Oh no! I rang. *Can you mute it?*

Luke punched a few buttons to try to silence the ringer but it was too late. Baldie had heard.

I peered over the edge of the slide and caught Baldie's eye. Darn. He smiled evilly and headed our way while he spoke into his phone. "One way or another, sit tight. This deal isn't over until I say it's over."

We need to split up to confuse him, I rang to Luke and cocked my head for him to head in the other direction.

Are you sure? Luke asked.

It's the only way.

Luke headed one way and I circled the pool going in the other direction. Baldie watched us both, holding his phone in one hand and pulling a wrench out of his pocket with the other.

"That alarm is for you by the way!" I called out, trying to rattle him. "There are policemen freeing that kid from cabin 1078 as we speak."

Baldie squinted his eyes and sneered. "That kid should'na been nosing around. Served him right for sneaking onto the ship like that."

"They're coming for you next," Luke called out from the other direction.

Baldie turned to Luke then snapped his head back toward me to keep an eye on us both.

Do you think he has a gun? I rang out to Luke.

I doubt he'd be waving a wrench around if he had a gun, Luke rang back.

Get the police up here, I rang to Luke.

I'm texting Trey on Bobbie's phone right now. He says they're on their way but are getting slowed down by the evacuating passengers.

"What's that sound?" Baldie shook his head. He must have caught a bit of our rings in between the intermittent alarm.

"Maybe you should get your ears checked once they put you in jail," Luke said.

"I hear they have great dental too," I added, giving Luke a chance to slip toward the gangway leading to the elevator doors. "And you can get a jail-yard tattoo of a merman while you're at it!"

Baldie's eyes popped open in surprise.

"What do you know about that?" he asked. Then a look of realization crossed his face. "That noise you two were making. That's the same noise Henry was making to his pals when I figured out his secret. You two little punks are mers too."

The guy is bright enough, I rang to Luke. *Too bad he hasn't used it for the power of good.*

Imagine what he could accomplish, Luke rang back with a laugh. By then, he'd made it to the gangway by the lifeboats, but he stayed put, texting something on his father's phone.

"What?" Baldie demanded. "What are you saying?"

"We're just saying how clever you are," I said, edging around the pool to keep a safe distance from his wrench. "Only you're not *so* clever because I'm the one who knows where that green backpack is and you don't."

Baldie's face hardened into an evil expression. He stalked toward me. "Why, you little brat. You're going to tell me where that backpack is or—"

"Or what?" I asked, circling the pool as he approached. "You're going to tell everyone my mer secret? You're about to get nailed for kidnapping a minor, buddy. Who's going to believe anything coming out of your mouth?"

"It sounds a little crazy and desperate if you ask me," Luke called out from across the deck to distract him.

Baldie turned toward Luke then back to me, trying to keep track of where we were. The sound of the alarm seemed to have him seriously spooked, though, because he turned toward the lifeboats to make his escape.

"I'm outta here," he yelled and grabbed Luke along the way. "And I'm taking you with me for insurance."

Mr. Martin's phone popped out of Luke's hand and skittered across the deck toward me. I ran to grab it.

"Wait!" I yelled. Adrenaline shot through my veins as I saw Luke struggle against Baldie. I tried to dial someone's number (anyone's!) but my fingers fumbled over the phone's screen. "Don't!"

But Baldie had already released the lever to lower the lifeboat to deck level and was forcing Luke inside.

"I told you! I know where the backpack is!" I yelled, stashing the phone in my bag and hoping Baldie wouldn't see. "Take me instead. I can show you!"

I knew it wasn't the smartest thing, trading one hostage for another, but I was the reason Luke was there in the first place. He'd said we should get the police right away back on the pier and I didn't listen. It was my fault Luke was in trouble.

"Maybe I should take both of you," Baldie said once he'd tied Luke's hands behind his back with rope from the lifeboat. "Yeah. That's what I'll do. Get in!"

"All right, all right," I said. "Just let him go."

"Do you think I'm an idiot?" he asked. "I said *get in*!"

I had to get Baldie away from Luke and give the police time to make it to the upper deck.

"You'll have to catch me first," I said, clutching my bag to my chest.

Jade, watch out! Luke rang.

Baldie lunged toward me with the wrench but slipped on the wet deck in the process. He gained his balance and chased me toward the bow. I ducked, avoiding the wrench as Baldie swung it my way. My only escape was to jump in the pool and run for the waterslide, trying not to get my bag and Mr. Martin's phone wet just in case I'd need it.

"Come back here," Baldie yelled, jumping into the pool to catch me. I didn't have a choice but to jump into the waterslide opening. I climbed up, up, up, trying to brace my feet and hands along the sides of the slide so I wouldn't slip back down. The tube slide was see-through so I could see Baldie fold his arms over his chest and laugh at me, thinking there was no way I was going to escape.

My head began to spin as I traveled through the tube,

moving across the ship's railing until I was hanging out over the side of the deck and looking down into the watery depths of the ocean. I stopped and braced myself against the slide, ignoring the fact that I was basically hovering hundreds of feet above the Atlantic Ocean.

Hurl alert!

It was true—I was trapped. But the smug look on Baldie's face made my blood boil. The guy had to pay for what he did. And Ensel too. Hopefully I'd stalled Baldie long enough for the cops to get here in time. What about Ensel, though? He couldn't walk free!

I took a deep breath and was focused on Baldie's terrible, self-satisfied face when I got an idea. I fished in my bag and pulled out Mr. Martin's phone and Ensel's business card. I punched in the number and started a new message.

I'm the guy with the stuff. Be at the drop site in half an hour.

Seconds later, a message popped up from Ensel.

You better not be messing with me. Got a lot riding on this deal.

I looked down the slide and saw that Baldie had decided I wasn't worth it because he was back at the lifeboat, lowering it with him and Luke inside. Oh no! He couldn't escape. Where were the cops?

I texted Trey and Cori at Bobbie's number.

almost here?

Seconds later, they texted back.

holdno! almst trhe!!

gr8! & get the cops to señor frg's in half an hour. anthr bad guy to arrest!

I was about to slide down the waterslide to try and stop Baldie when two policemen rushed onto the deck. They stopped the lifeboat's descent and nabbed Baldie. Trey and Cori arrived moments later with the lady officer. While she helped get Luke untied, he looked my way and flashed an adorable "We did it!" smile.

I held a finger up to my lips so he wouldn't let on I was there.

I had a backpack to deliver.

Chapter Nineteen

ONCE BALDIE WAS ARRESTED and they took him away, I waited until everyone was long gone and then slid back down the waterslide. I rushed down the stairs and back onto the dock, far away from prying eyes, then took a huge swan dive into the harbor.

I hit the water so hard that I saw white. Then my legs exploded into a tail as my sundress swirled around me.

I spun around toward the pier, working the muscles of my newly formed tail, and swept my arms behind me to get some momentum. It was completely dark by then—I guessed it was about 10 p.m.—making it hard to see through the gloomy water, but my eyes had adjusted to the dark by the time I reached the pier.

The backpack. Where was it? I traveled up and down along the pier, trying to remember exactly where I'd stashed it. Then I remembered that Henry was toward the bow of the cruise ship when I found him, not the stern, so I swam under the ship's hull to the other side and kept swimming, hunting around the framework of the pier.

After ten minutes or so of searching, I started to panic. What if I couldn't find the backpack? What if Ensel got away with his dirty tricks? He'd probably make up some kind of story about Dillon and pin everything on Baldie. Who would believe a proven kidnapper like Baldie over a police officer like Ensel? I couldn't let Ensel just walk away.

Finally, I saw a flash of green a few dozen feet down the pier. The backpack!

I swam to it and pulled it off the spike where I'd left it, scraping my hand in the process.

Yeowch! Pain sliced across my palm, and my arm almost snapped off as the backpack sank like a boulder to the bottom of the ocean.

I swam after it and struggled to slip the bag onto my back along with my own backpack, and then I remembered I still had Mr. Martin's phone in there. Oops. Being a mermaid definitely wasn't electronics friendly.

My hand ached from scraping it on the sharp spike, and the weight of Baldie's backpack pulled me down to the ocean floor. I pushed my swaying hair away from my face and struggled to keep moving, but I felt like I was carrying a hundred-pound sack of potatoes. One way or another, though, I had to get to Señor Frog's.

I swam with all my might, but the weight of the backpack slowed me to the speed of a one-armed dog paddle.

By then, I was sure I'd been in the water for at least twenty minutes and I was barely skimming the bottom of the ocean floor with my feeble swimming attempts. At the rate I was going, it would take me well into next week to get to the drop-off.

I wasn't sure if it was the hopelessness of the situation,

knowing there was no way I'd make it to Señor Frog's on time, but the evening light dimmed even more than usual, casting dark shadows all around me. It didn't help that my hand was now throbbing. And, ugh, was it bleeding?

I looked up, wondering if a cloud had covered the moon, and saw the most terrifying thing I'd ever seen.

Edges of moonlight glistened around an unmistakable sleek, dark shadow.

Slow moving. Stealthy. Sharp finned.

Shark! I rang out without thinking.

The shark zoomed toward me, sensing my presence, probably sniffing the blood from my hand. I swam with all my might, desperate to get away, with the soundtrack from Cori's video blaring in my head.

I'm sorry, Cori! I should have gone shark diving with you! Now I have no shark skills, and it's all my fault! I rang, nearly delirious with fear.

I felt something grip the back of my backpack with such force that it snapped my head back.

Ack! I couldn't believe it. After months and months as a mermaid, I was about to become a mer-kebab!

The great reef tiger shark (or whatever the monster with the death grip on my backpack was called) shook me back and forth through the water like a toddler swinging a rag doll.

I am SO dead, I rang.

But all of a sudden, I felt a thump from behind. I swung my head around and caught a glimpse of a second shadow. Then a third.

Thump! Thump!

Ocean human! I heard a ring call.

The dolphins!

The water around me filled with the loudest, shriekiest sounds I'd ever heard as the dolphins called to one another. Within seconds, more dolphins appeared all around me, adding to the noise.

Thump! Thump!

The dolphins were attacking the shark! They were trying to save me.

I covered my ears and squeezed my eyes shut as the noise and force of the fight behind me intensified. The shark kept swinging me around, making my brain scramble inside my skull.

Thump! Thump! Thump!

Finally, thankfully, amazingly, the shark let go and I floated down, down, down to the bottom of the ocean, exhausted by the fight and weighed down by the backpack. I landed face up, looking up at the battle in the water above me as the dolphins rammed into the shark, chasing it away.

I could barely move, barely process what had just happened, barely believe I was still alive!

Seconds later, the same silver-beaked dolphin I'd seen at the marina the night before appeared by my side in the moonlight.

It's you! I rang, relieved to see a friendly face. Um, beak. I tried to speak as plainly as possible so the dolphin could understand. *You saved me! Thank you!*

You help ocean human. Make harbor safe for us again. We help you. The dolphin motioned with his beak for his friend to come nearer. At first, the other dolphin was skittish but I must have looked pretty harmless because soon he came to my side.

You mean Henry? I asked. *He's okay now. He'll be going home soon so you can have your harbor back. But I need to catch the bad human who hurt him.*

And by "human" I meant Ensel, though he was pretty *sub*human as far as I was concerned. I was fairly sure Ensel didn't know anything about mers—Baldie had told him his "guy" was a scuba diver, not a mer—but clearly Ensel was as much to blame for Henry's situation as Baldie was.

Bad human? the dolphin replied.

Yes. I struggled to get moving again, hoping the shark hadn't torn too big a hole in the backpack. *I need to get this bag somewhere very soon or else the bad human will escape.*

We help you again, then no more ocean humans? the dolphin asked.

So they wanted me gone too? I guess I was only slightly less irritating to be around than a full-fledged mer, but I tried not to take it personally that I was still rather offensive.

Trust me, I rang back. *The sooner I get out of this harbor, the better!*

Then, we go! The dolphin and his friend each grabbed a strap of the backpack and pulled me along while their pals formed a dolphin guard all around me in case the shark came back.

Okay, then, if you insist! I rang, letting them drag my limp, tired body in the general direction of the Straw Market. *Off to Señor Frog's!*

Thankfully, the big yellow hook attached to the pier below Señor Frog's was fairly easy to find once we got there, but if Officer Ensel wanted the stash in the backpack, he'd have to get very wet. I attached the bag to the hook and gave the straps a few extra turns and knots, just to make things interesting. The pack had a rip at the top of the bag, thanks to my toothy pal, but none of the load was lost as far as I could tell. Though I shuddered at the thought of what could have happened to me if I hadn't been carrying smuggled goods on my back.

I said good-bye to my dolphin friends and swam to the far end of the wharf, hidden from view, so I could watch what was going on without being seen while my tail transformed back to legs. I took a few deep breaths of air and tried not to cough as it burned down my throat. Music played from inside the restaurant, but there was still no sign of Officer Ensel.

Soon, my tail started to burn with its own heat, and I knew that it was only a matter of minutes before it started dissolving into legs. My eyes stung with tears as I forced myself not to cry out in pain, but the more I forced the pain away, the more it kept coming. I could barely keep from screaming when I saw him.

Carl Ensel.

He'd stripped down to his boxer shorts and was climbing down the ladder near the hook. At first I don't think he saw the bag, but soon he spotted it and climbed a bit farther down into the water to try and reach it. Thankfully, my legs had fully formed by then and my fancy knot handiwork gave me a few extra minutes to get myself out of the water to check and see if the police had arrived yet.

The coast was still clear, so I hobbled barefoot toward where Officer Ensel was retrieving the backpack, keeping close to a small shed near the water's edge and out of sight. The patio of Señor Frog's was on the other side of the shed so the customers couldn't see me, but still, I didn't want to have to explain why a fourteen-year-old girl was walking around barefoot in a dripping-wet sundress in the middle of the night.

"Oof." I almost tripped on Ensel's clothes as I sneaked around the shed. When I realized what they were, a smile grew on my lips. I picked up the clothes and bundled them in my arms. When I heard a jingle, I realized it must be Ensel's keys! I slipped those into the pocket of my sundress for safe keeping.

I could hear Officer Ensel cursing as he kept trying to untie the backpack, so I took the time to plot what to do with his clothes and smiled at the thought of him stuck in his boxers.

But where were the police? I wondered. I tried Mr. Martin's phone from my backpack, but it was fried. I checked the pockets of Ensel's pants for a phone. Nothing.

Maybe he'd left it in his car, but I had no idea what his car looked like. I could only hope that Cori and Trey got the message to the police and they arrived in time to catch Officer Ensel red-handed.

"Got it," I heard Ensel whisper to himself.

Ensel's head popped up over the pier as he climbed the ladder and struggled with the water-logged backpack. I looked all around me, trying to see if the police had arrived yet, but I couldn't see anyone. I slipped behind the shed, watching Ensel as he hunted around for his clothes. After a few minutes, he gave up and started to leave. He probably wouldn't get very far without his keys, but I couldn't take the chance that he would escape with the evidence.

"Yoo-hoo!" I called out from behind the shed as I dangled his pants in the air. "Looking for these?"

Ensel looked my way. The nearby streetlamp was enough to show the shocked look on his face.

"Where did you get those? Give those back, you little brat!" He started toward me, but I threw the pants at him to slow him down. He picked them up and put them on hastily, giving me enough time to run back a few dozen feet, closer to the stalls of the Straw Market. I slipped into the maze of stalls, trying to hide as Ensel approached. I could hear him on the other side of the stalls' canvas walls, cursing as he walked along the uneven gravel.

"You're that girl who was with Dillon on Monday, aren't you?" Ensel called out. "Good thing he made it back home okay, isn't it?"

His words rang with a false note, like an actor trying too hard to convince you of his part.

I waited until he'd passed the booth where I was hiding before answering. "We both know Dillon didn't make it home."

There was silence on the other side of the canvas for a moment, and then his voice pierced the dark night.

"It would be a real shame if you didn't make it home either," Ensel replied.

A chill ran through me.

I backtracked along the stalls in the opposite direction, knowing there was an opening where I'd popped out to see Dillon's shells back on Monday. I hung on to Ensel's shirt and shoes and tried my best not to trip. I peered around the corner of the canvas to catch a glimpse of him and saw that he was about thirty feet away, pulling back the canvas of the stalls to look inside. Now that he knew that I knew he had something to do with Dillon's disappearance, there was no way he was leaving without getting the whole story.

"I know about your pal over at Wonderment Cruiselines too, you jerk!" I yelled, throwing a shoe out into the water to confuse him. Ensel spun around, trying to make out the source of the splash as I ducked back into the stalls and cut across to the opening on the other side of the tent. I checked to see if the cops had arrived yet, but there were still no flashing lights to be seen. I doubled back, dashing down the side of the tent toward Señor Frog's, hoping to buy a little more time.

"I'm clean." Officer Ensel's sinister voice rang through the air. I couldn't tell where it was coming from because it was so dark, but he was close. Very close. "Nobody can pin anything on me about that kid. Now give me my keys!"

"Ahh!" I yelled as Ensel jumped out from behind the canvas tent and lunged toward me. I threw his shirt over his head to distract him then made a break for it. That's when a set of headlights whizzed toward me and screeched to a stop in front of the Straw Market.

"Faye!" I recognized the taxi van right away. She jumped out and ran after Ensel, brandishing her handbag.

"Yeah, you *better* run, Carl Jr.!" she yelled at him as Ensel ran off, toting the backpack on his shoulder. "Wait till I tell your mama what you been up to, terrorizing little girls! You should be ashamed of yourself."

The flashing lights of a police cruiser came from the other direction and screeched to a stop in front of Señor Frog's, trapping Ensel against the outdoor patio as Faye hurled insults and swung her handbag at him from the other direction. Two police officers jumped out of their cruiser, and soon Ensel was on his knees with the backpack on the ground and his hands over his head.

I clutched Ensel's other shoe to my chest as everyone else piled out of Faye's van. There were Mom and Dad, the Martins, the Blakes, and Cori, Trey, and Luke.

"Oh my gosh," I said, trying to keep from shaking as they huddled around me to see if I was okay. I wasn't sure if it was because I was still drying off from being wet or because of what had just happened, but I welcomed the sweater Dad draped around my shoulders just as the police slapped handcuffs on Ensel and read him his rights.

"I'm guessing your hair isn't wet because you forgot to dry it after your shower," Dad said.

"Yeah, about that…" I began.

"Cori, Luke, and Trey explained everything," Mom said.

"So you're not mad?" I asked.

"Oh, I'm *plenty* mad," Dad replied. "But first, are you okay?"

"Yeah, I'm okay," I said.

I guess that gave him license to go off on me because I listened for a full five minutes to his rant about how we'd come to the Bahamas to *relax*, not to get drawn into another mer fiasco, and how could I worry my mother like that and did I know there are *sharks* off the coast of Paradise Island?

"Thanks for the reminder, Dad," I muttered, with the memory of my good buddy shark-a-doodle dancing in my head. But, I didn't think it was the right time to bring that up. Maybe another time. Another lifetime!

"The point is, you have no idea what's underwater here in the Bahamas! Are you crazy, swimming around here like that?"

"It was for a good cause," I said hopefully, pointing to the police cruiser. "Look, we caught the bad guy."

Just then, Faye arrived, still brandishing her handbag at Ensel as the police shut the cruiser's back door on him.

Mom gave Dad a warning look to get him to shush, so we didn't spill our mer secret to Faye.

"We'll talk about this later," Dad muttered.

"The absolute nerve of that man," Faye said when she finally calmed down after the police cruiser drove away. "First he helps kidnap poor Dillon. Then Cori tells me he takes Jade here on a wild boat ride around the harbor."

Ah, so that's the story Cori made up. Good girl.

"Did he hurt you?" Faye asked.

"No, I'm fine," I assured her.

"Well, let's get everyone home," Faye said as she headed for the van. "I hear tomorrow's the big day and everyone needs their beauty sleep."

"It *has* been a long day," Mom said as she held the door of the van for me to climb inside.

"No joke," I replied, collapsing into the seat next to Luke. He put his arm around me (very good sign!) while Dad gave him the evil eye.

"Not now, Dad," I said, resting my head on Luke's shoulder and fighting to keep my eyes open after a fun-filled evening of dragging my tail along the Bahamian coastline.

The last thing I remembered about that night was a big green frog in a sombrero waving to us as we pulled away.

Chapter Twenty

F IVE DOLLARS EACH. THREE for fifteen!" I called out from Dillon's colorful blanket, surrounded by white and coral conches. The warm Caribbean sun made the shells sparkle, and a brisk wind carried the salty scent of the ocean from the harbor.

Rayelle's mom had gotten Raymond to tow Dillon's boat back to the Straw Market with his water taxi. She'd set up the blanket with his shells next to her booth, and Rayelle, Cori, and I spent Saturday morning manning Dillon's Treasures while Dillon was being kept at the hospital for observation.

"Dillon should really think about adjusting his sale prices," Cori joked after she finished packing up a conch for a middle-aged couple with matching fanny packs.

"I dunno," I replied, picking up one of the conches and admiring the pearly interior of the shell. "You know what they say—you get what you pay for, and these are pretty awesome."

Looking at the conches just added to the happy feeling of knowing Baldie and Ensel were safely behind bars, Eddie and Bobbie had a plan to sail back to Florida with Henry, and Mom and Dad were (hopefully) getting married that night.

"So," Rayelle said, looking up from a message on her phone. She'd been texting with Dillon all morning while he waited for the doctor to release him from the hospital. "Word on the street is that Ensel's backpack was filled with cold medicine."

"Cold medicine? Is it flu season in the Bahamas or something?" I asked.

"No," Rayelle said. "They use the chemicals in the medicine to make a dangerous kind of street drug called Grip."

"Wow, can you believe all this?" I said to Cori. Sure, it was only shrink-wrapped, waterproof cold medicine when I dragged the backpack across Nassau Harbor, but I shuddered at the thought of how dangerous the cargo could be once the drug dealers got hold of it and transformed it into something much more potent.

"Unbelievable. And scary." Cori said.

"Oh my gosh." Rayelle put a hand to her mouth as she continued reading Dillon's message.

"What?" I asked.

"Dillon had told me Charla and her friends were bad news, but I had no idea this was all going on. Look!"

Dillon admitted to Rayelle that he had worked as a messenger for the group of kids who sold necklaces at the Straw Market. The same group who gave us a hard time earlier that week. Only, the necklaces were just a cover-up for dealing Grip.

"Now I know how that girl could afford such expensive accessories!" Cori exclaimed as we kept reading Dillon's text over Rayelle's shoulder.

"He says he stopped being the gang's messenger once he figured out what they were really up to. He even helped Kiki's boyfriend, John, get clean when John almost lost his job at Dolphin Lagoon for being high. But Dillon had no idea Ensel was behind it all," Rayelle continued as she texted a message back to Dillon.

"That Ensel guy was a real jerk, huh?" I said.

"Not exactly in the running for Cop of the Month," Cori agreed.

"So…" I said to Rayelle. "Your mom seems to have had a change of heart about Dillon."

I stole a glance at her mom as she worked on a straw hat. She caught my eye and smiled.

"Yeah," Rayelle whispered, looking up from her phone. "I told her about how Dillon helped me last year. She's kind of coming around."

"So are you guys going to start dating or something?" I asked, trying to get the dirt.

"I'm not sure," Rayelle said shyly. "We'll see."

"Well, he'd be crazy not to ask you out," Cori said.

I looked at Cori and laughed. "I thought you were on the brink of giving up on guys for good."

"What can I say—I'm a hopeless romantic at heart," Cori said.

We hung out for another hour or so and sold a few more shells, but all too soon it was time to head back to the hotel so we could get ready for the big night.

"Okay, so we've sold ten of Dillon's shells and there are

six left," Rayelle said, counting up the money. "It won't make up for missing a whole week of sales, but hopefully it helps."

"Thank you, honey," Rayelle's mom said with a grateful smile as she tucked the money into an outside pocket of her money belt. "I'll be sure he gets it."

"So what do we do with the rest of these?" Cori said, motioning to the shells. "Should we put them back on his boat?"

"Well, I can either buy that 'It's Better in the Bahamas' T-shirt I saw earlier or clean out Dillon's stock for tonight's festivities." I pulled out my wallet and counted thirty dollars to put with the rest of the money for Dillon.

"Good choice," Rayelle said as she helped us pack up the rest of the shells and take them to the water taxi.

Raymond was waiting for us at the dock. He took the bag from Rayelle as we stepped into the taxi boat, and all of a sudden a wave of sadness washed over me, knowing I would be leaving the Bahamas in the morning and heading back to Port Toulouse. What would be waiting for me when I arrived back home? Rumors? Whispers? Sidelong glances?

And what was I leaving behind? Sun and surf? But more than that. New friends. Great friends. Faye. Dillon. And Rayelle.

"Hey, Rayelle," I said as I stepped into the water taxi. "My mom and dad are having their wedding party tonight. Why don't you come with your grandma? Bring Dillon too if he gets out of the hospital in time."

"Wouldn't miss it," Rayelle said with a wave and a beaming smile as the taxi pulled away from the pier.

"What a crazy week," I said, flopping onto my bed once Cori and I got back from the Straw Market. "I thought the Mermish Council thing this summer was whacked, but this week could have ended really badly. Especially for Dillon."

"I'm really sorry I gave you such a hard time about the whole Dillon thing," Cori said. "Count that as a total fail for me in the friend department."

"Hey, you're still staying here with me at the Asylum while your mom and dad are living it up at the Eutopia. If that doesn't prove your friendship, I'm not sure what does," I joked.

"Yeah, but you knew something was wrong, and I kept trying to blow it off."

"Well, to be fair, I thought I was going a little crazy too," I replied.

"But I made it seem like you were being paranoid because of everything you've been through this summer when it was the opposite," Cori added. "You, my friend, have excellent merma-drama radar."

"Merma-drama radar?" I asked with a laugh.

"Built-in radar for mermaid drama. It's your super-power," Cori said.

"Maybe I should get *that* on a T-shirt," I joked.

"Well, actually…" Cori got a sly look on her face and pulled something out of her bag. "It's not the same but I hope you like it. Just a little something to thank you for such an awesome week."

It was a neon blue T-shirt with white lettering that said *Mermaid Hair, Just Don't Care.* And just my size!

"I love it!" I said, pulling it on over my tank top. "But you realize I won't be able to set foot outside in this thing, right?"

Cori laughed. "I wouldn't set foot outside in that thing either, but mostly because it doesn't match anything I own."

Luke and Trey arrived just then. Things had been so crazy, I wasn't sure where the Cori-Trey thing stood after their squabble the night before. And if the Cori-Trey thing was weird, would that make things weird for the Jade-Luke thing?

"Hey," I said as I answered the door.

"We have arrived!" Trey exclaimed, diving onto my bed to grab the TV remote. Soon, *Flunky and Blob* cartoons were blaring in the background.

"Nice shirt!" Luke said as he sat beside his brother. "So, you guys all ready for the big day?"

"I think so," I said, going to Mom and Dad's door. "I should check if my parents need anything."

"If they can hear you knock over the sound of the TV." Cori rolled her eyes at Trey as she went into the bathroom to brush her teeth.

So, the Cori-Trey thing wasn't quite back online apparently. Dad answered the door.

"Hey, Jade," Dad said as he popped his head in through the doorway. When he spotted Luke and Trey, his face took on a four-star general look and his voice dipped an octave. "Hello, boys."

"Hello, Mr. Baxter," Luke and Trey said in unison over the *Flunky and Blob* laugh track.

"Dude," Luke whispered to Trey as he wrestled the remote from him and turned down the volume on the TV.

Dad sneaked a glance over his shoulder at his room, making me wonder if something was wrong.

"Is everything okay?" I asked.

"It's just…we got a call from the hotel catering staff. Because of all the other weddings and our last-minute plans, they can't make the sushi I special-ordered for your mom and the cake is a no go. Your mom is on the phone trying to order another cake right now, but it doesn't look good. Plus, we still won't know about the officiate until the last minute, and there's no way the flute player can make it because she was double-booked with another wedding at the Eutopia—"

"Dad! Slow down," I said, grasping his arm. The guy was wound up tighter than a ball of Gran's yarn. This was no way for Mom and Dad to spend their last day in the Bahamas, worrying about whether or not they could get California rolls for their beachside wedding. I owed it to them to take their mind off their troubles, so I looked around the room at Cori, Trey, and Luke, thinking up a plan.

If the four of us could stop an international drug-smuggling operation, surely we could help Mom and Dad on their special day. "Tell you what—why don't you guys chill out for the afternoon? What's done is done, and I'm sure it's all going to work out."

"I don't know…" Dad looked over his shoulder again to where Mom was on hold with the cake people. It killed me to see the pained look on her face on what was *supposed* to be one of the happiest days of her life.

"Well, *I* know," I said, going into their room and taking the phone from Mom to hang it up. "Mom. Call Bobbie, Mrs. Blake, and Mrs. Martin. You guys are going to the spa for the afternoon. Dad, get the guys on the phone. There are four of you, right? Perfect for a golf foursome. Make it happen!"

Luke, Trey, and Cori stood at the door to our room and nodded in agreement.

"But there's so much to do!" Mom said, tucking her hair behind her ear. "The food, the music…"

I looked at all my friends, and Luke smiled at me, realizing I had a plan brewing. We may end up with Cheez-Its and our best rendition of "Gangnam Style" for music, but I knew, despite our disagreements, that if anyone could come up with a solution to Mom and Dad's last-minute worries, it was the four of us.

"Leave it to us," I replied with a smile.

Cori and Trey decided they were in charge of music because apparently I have no taste in music, so I decided I'd take care of snacks with Luke because that was an area I definitely excelled in.

While Cori and Trey went back to the Eutopia to make a wedding playlist on Trey's iPod and hopefully find a docking station to amplify the music, Luke and I headed to a food market a half mile down the road.

"Okay, so we have potato chips, pretzels, paper plates, napkins…" I looked in my basket to take inventory and sighed.

"What's the matter?" Luke asked.

"I just don't know if this is going to cut it," I replied. "I was really hoping there would be more dessert stuff to choose from since they don't have a cake, but without an oven or a stove to prepare anything fancier, this looks like the best we're going to do."

"I'm sure it'll be great," Luke said. But I could tell he was still hunting around the market shelves for something better.

"Yeah, but it's just such a far cry from what my parents ordered earlier this week. My dad had even arranged for my mom's favorite sushi as a treat, since she loves seafood so much," I said.

Luke got a look in his eyes, and I followed him two aisles down where he picked up a box of Rice Crispies.

"Sushi, huh?" he asked. I followed him to the next aisle, where he grabbed marshmallows and a box of Fruit Roll-Ups. "Trey has this thing he made for a bake sale once. Do you guys have a microwave in your room? And a fridge?"

"Yeah…" I said slowly. "Why?"

"Well then, I've got you covered," Luke replied, tossing a final bag in the basket as we got to the cashier. "As long as your mom doesn't mind gummy worms in her sushi."

Chapter Twenty-One

B Y THE TIME EVERYONE gathered at the gazebo on the beach below the Alyssum Hotel at sunset, the wind had died down and a light tropical breeze had replaced it.

Mom and Dad were still getting ready back at the hotel. Everyone else chipped in to decorate and get chairs and a table down to the gazebo since there was no hotel staff to help us. Town Hall had never called us back, so the mood was a lot less festive than we'd planned. We tried to make the best of things, though, and laid out the snacks and drinks and Trey's special "sushi" that Luke and I had made that afternoon.

"Hey, those turned out pretty well!" I exclaimed to Luke as guests kept nabbing the sushi treats, which consisted of gummy worms surrounded by marshmallow Rice Crispies and wrapped in green Fruit Roll-Up "seaweed."

"Trey made them when our mom told him he had to do his own baking for the skate-park bake sale since he waited until the last minute to tell her about it. I'm telling you—they sold like hot cakes."

"Leave it to Trey," I said with a laugh.

Rayelle and Dillon arrived just then, and I crossed the gazebo to meet them.

"You came!" I exclaimed and gave Rayelle a hug. I didn't

care if I barely knew the guy, but I gave Dillon a huge hug too. "I'm so glad you're okay."

"Thanks," Dillon said, putting an arm around Rayelle. I snuck a glance at her and gave her a "way to go" eyebrow wiggle. She beamed. "Rayelle told me everything you did for me. I just wanted to make sure I could say thank you before you left to go back home."

"I'm sorry I didn't have your back from the very beginning," I said. "I made up my mind about you before giving you a chance."

"Well," Dillon said with a wry smile, "it's not like I'm some kind of saint or anything. And anyway, I was the one who was wrong about you."

"You mean I'm not a princess after all?" I said with a laugh.

"Well, maybe a mob princess with the way you took down that cop!" Dillon joked. By then, a few people came over to introduce themselves to Dillon and wish him well.

I turned to Rayelle. "Hey, where's your grandma?"

"Oh, she just has to get something from the van. She'll be here in a few minutes," Rayelle said with a vague wave of her hand.

Cori switched the music on Trey's iPod to something more wedding-y when we spotted Mom and Dad coming down the steps from the hotel onto the boardwalk to the gazebo.

"Wow, she looks so pretty," Cori whispered to me as she placed the iPod in a bowl to try and amplify the sound. She and Trey hadn't had any luck tracking down an iPod docking station, so that was the best they could do.

"She really does look beautiful," I agreed.

Mom wore a hand-crocheted, antique-white slip dress, and her newly styled hair was perfect with the shell hairpins we'd found at the Straw Market earlier that week. Dad wore his tropical shirt and straw hat, but instead of looking touristy, he actually looked pretty handsome. The goofy sock tan that cut across his legs midcalf didn't really add to the effect, but the fact he was barefoot along with the rest of the party guests proved how much this vacation had given him the rest and relaxation he and Mom so truly deserved.

Mom and Dad greeted their guests as they arrived at the gazebo. The Blakes, the Martins, and Bobbie and Eddie were all there. I looked for Trey, but he wasn't with his parents.

"Hello, everyone," Dad said as he handed out champagne and sparkling water. "Micci and I really want to thank you for making the trip to the Bahamas with us. You all know what this means to us, and even though it looks like things aren't going to work out with the wedding…" This is where Dad kind of lost it a little and Mom jumped in to finish.

"What Dalrymple is trying to say is that we consider each and every one of you a part of our family, and even though we can't make our own family official yet"— Mom looked at me and smiled— "this is more than enough for now."

Everyone raised their glasses in a toast, and Dad and Mom came over to give me a big hug. I really couldn't imagine being happier than just then—knowing that our family was safe and intact again. Sure, it would have been nice to head back to Port Toulouse officially a family, but looking around at Bobbie and Eddie, at Cori and her parents, Luke and his parents, and knowing that Gran was back in Port Toulouse thinking of us, that was all I needed.

Someone was missing, though.

"Where *is* Trey, anyway?" I asked Cori once the toasts were done. "I wanted him to get some of the Rice Crispy sushi treats before they're all gone."

"We got in a big fight about the music because I told him we should put Taylor 'n Tyler's 'Make Me Wanna Fly' on the playlist. He said the song was stupid, and I told him I couldn't believe he didn't remember that song was playing the first time we went to the skate park together. He can't even remember *our* song."

"*You make me...*" I heard the familiar song fill the air and turned to see where it was coming from. Had the frat boys turned up the volume on the music around the pool? "*You make me wanna fly...*"

That's when I saw Taylor 'n Tyler walking down the steps from the hotel to the beach, hand in hand. They harmonized their hit song together as they approached the gazebo, followed by Trey.

"What's going on?" I turned to Cori and whispered. But Cori had her hands to her mouth and her eyes were shining as if she was on the verge of tears. That's when I realized—Trey had somehow convinced Taylor 'n Tyler to come serenade Mom and Dad on their wedding day to make up for everything with Cori.

"You make me wanna fly,
So high, so high,
Like bubbles in the sky..."

Faye arrived right behind them, blowing bubbles from a small container. Taylor handed out more bubble containers to the rest of the guests from a basket she was carrying, and soon we were all blowing bubbles and the sky was filled with wispy globes of awesome.

Tyler held out his hand to help Faye into the gazebo. It seemed so natural for her to be there, considering everything we'd been through that week, but I was a bit confused by the official-looking book Faye was holding.

"Dearly beloved..." Faye held out her arms to get everyone's attention. "We are gathered here today to join this man and this woman."

"Pardon?" My dad turned to Faye, wondering what she was doing.

"Surprise!" a voice called out, and I realized it came from the iPad Trey was holding. It was Gran, joining the party via Skype.

"Trey!" Cori gushed. "You did all this?"

"I'll take credit for the iPad, but Taylor 'n Tyler volunteered when I explained the situation with the bumped reservation," Trey said, popping a sushi snack in his mouth. Cori hugged him and whispered something in his ear, which sounded like an apology for being so hard on him.

"And my grandma has been working to renew her officiate's license all week since she heard about the wedding,"

Rayelle chimed in. "She just didn't want to get anyone's hopes up."

Faye gathered Mom and Dad at the front of the gazebo, and Mom reached out her hand for me to join them. Faye opened the ceremony with a beautiful poem about the infinity of love and oceans, followed by the more formal part of the ceremony with words like "love" and "trust" and "commitment."

By the time Mom and Dad were ready to exchange their vows, a lump the size of a golf ball had lodged itself in my throat and I had to squeeze my eyes shut for a second to keep from crying.

"Dalrymple," Mom began. "We may have gone through life so far without a paper to prove how committed we are to each other, but from the first day we met, your spirit belonged to me and mine to you in a way no ceremony could define."

Dad wiped his cheek and joined his hands with Mom's once more. "Michaela. Whoever thought a guy like me could be lucky enough to not only love a woman like you but have that love returned to him tenfold? You are my life, my love, my forever."

By then, everyone was pulling tissues out of their handbags or blinking uncontrollably. I caught Cori clutching a bottle of bubbles to her chest, hanging on every word, while Gran peeped out from the iPad, blowing her nose in a big hankie.

"Michaela and Dalrymple," Faye said, "with these vows, you have dedicated yourselves to one another and have agreed to live together in matrimony. I now pronounce you—husband and wife."

Mom and Dad looked at each other for a moment then laughed, not really knowing what to do next.

"Well, go on!" Faye said to Dad. "Kiss your bride!"

It was dark and the moon was out by the time the wedding was over, and the hotel finally delivered the food for our afterparty. Everyone stood around the gazebo chatting, eating, and drinking, and the sound of happy laughter filled the air. Luke came to find me and took my hand to lead me down the gazebo stairs to the beach.

"Where are we going?" I asked.

"I thought we'd gather some intel before we headed back to Port Toulouse," Luke said. "They've been talking for over half an hour. Who knows what we've missed already?"

That's when I spotted Trey and Cori sitting on the boardwalk.

"Should we really be spying on them?" I asked, a guilty feeling accumulating in my chest as we hid behind one of the pillars supporting the gazebo overhead.

"How else are we going to get the story on those two?" Luke asked. Then he produced something wrapped in a napkin for me. "Plus, I brought snacks. It was the last one."

"Candy sushi...you really know the way to a girl's heart," I said, taking a bite.

Shh, Luke rang to me. *We're missing all the good stuff.*

"That was really sweet of you with the music, Trey," Cori said from a few dozen feet away on the boardwalk.

"Yeah, but I'll have you know—that romantic stuff isn't normal for me," Trey said. "But that's what you deserve, Cori. Not the goofball I've been lately."

"That's just it, though. I *like* that you're a goofball," Cori said. "I'm just not sure that's what I want in a boyfriend."

"And I don't know if I can be the kind of boyfriend you want," Trey replied. "So does that move me into the friend zone, then?"

"I'm not sure," Cori said, and I could tell from the sound of her voice that this was hard for her.

"'Cause that's cool if that's the way it's gotta be," Trey said. "I just want to stop ticking you off all the time."

Cori was silent for a moment. "And I want to stop being ticked off at you for just being you. So yeah, I think the friend zone might be better."

"Cool," Trey said.

"Up high?" Cori raised her hand and gave Trey a high five. They hugged it out then stood up and joined everyone back in the gazebo.

"Well, there you have it," Luke said as we emerged from under the gazebo and continued walking down the beach.

"Is that going to be weird?" I asked. "Cori and Trey being just friends?"

"Weird how?" Luke asked as we reached the water and waded in up to our ankles.

"I dunno. Now that they're just friends, does that change anything for us?" I asked.

"Well…" Luke said in a teasing voice as he grasped me by the waist. "We can be 'just friends' too if you *really* want to."

"Are we talking friends-friends or kissy-friends?" I whispered as he pulled me close.

"Oh, definitely kissy-friends," Luke said, glancing up at the moon. "Wouldn't want to waste this perfect opportunity."

That's when Luke finally kissed me under the moonlight, making everything that had happened that week fall away.

"I'm kind of digging this kissy-friends status," I murmured between kisses, our foreheads touching.

"Me too," Luke replied.

New friends, old friends, new beginnings, fresh starts. Wasn't that what life was all about?

And to top it all off, I think I saw a dolphin jump out over the water in the moonlight just as Luke leaned in for another kiss.

If I could get all *that* on a T-shirt, I totally would.

Trey's Gummy Worm Sushi

Y OU DON'T NEED to like fish to like sushi!

Here's what you'll need:
- 4 tablespoons butter
- 4 cups mini marshmallows
- 6 cups crispy rice cereal
- 20 gummy worms
- 2 boxes of green Fruit Roll-Ups (for the seaweed!)

Plus:
- 12 x 17" cookie sheet lined with wax paper
- nonstick cooking spray

In the microwave:
1. Melt the butter in a microwaveable bowl for about 10 seconds (or until completely melted).
2. In a separate bowl, melt the marshmallows for 30 seconds at a time until completely melted, stirring each time you take the bowl out of the microwave.

Then:
1. Add the butter to the marshmallow mixture and stir.

2. Add the crispy rice cereal one cup at a time to the marsh-mallow/butter mixture and stir until well blended.
3. Spray the wax paper with nonstick cooking spray.
4. Pour out the cereal/marshmallow mixture onto the wax paper and flatten it to about 1 inch thick with a greased rolling pin (or your hands if you don't mind getting sticky!).
5. Let the rice crispy treat mixture cool.
6. Working from the short end of the baking sheet, place a line of gummy worms across the rice crispy treats, about an inch from the edge.
7. Using the wax paper to help, roll the rice crispy treats around the gummy worms once, so it will form a log, pressing it tightly so it will stick together.
8. Cut the log away from the rest of the pan and set aside.
9. Repeat with another line of gummy worms and roll and cut until you've used up all the rice crispy treats.
10. Slice off sushi rolls from the log one inch at a time then wrap in one-inch strips of green Fruit Roll-Up.

Then:
1. STUFF YOUR FACE

—Trey

Acknowledgments

Writing a book is a lot like being stuck on a deserted tropical island with circling sharks, but it is a process made much easier with the help of keen-eyed critique pals and super-patient friends and family.

Much thanks to my agent, Lauren MacLeod, for answering my smoke signals and helping me navigate through shark-infested waters as I took these scribblings from a vague idea to an actual book. Thanks also to my editor, Aubrey Poole, who always provides a safe place to land on shore and who helps make all my words shipshape with her expert editorial eye.

Marcelle, Charlotte, and Gord: you are my constant sources of support and inspiration. None of this happens without you.

About the Author

Hélène Boudreau never spotted a real mermaid while growing up on an island surrounded by the Atlantic Ocean, but she believes mermaids are just as plausible as giant squids, flying fish, or electric eels. She now writes fiction and nonfiction for kids from her landlocked home in Ontario, Canada. Her first book of this series, *Real Mermaids Don't Wear Toe Rings*, was a 2011 finalist for the Society of Children's Book Writers and Illustrators' Crystal Kite Award.

You can visit her at www.heleneboudreau.com.

Catch up on all of Jade's mer-adventures!

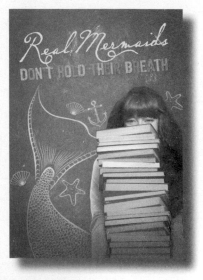